GOLD TO

Luke Tallon had been very good to Janna when she was virtually stranded in South America, and she would always be grateful to him. She knew, too, that she would always love him. But she could never expect him to love her in return—for he belonged to Annabel, the fiancée who was waiting for him in England . . .

GOLD TO REMEMBER

BY

MARY WIBBERLEY

MILLS & BOON LIMITED
15–16 BROOK'S MEWS
LONDON W1A 1DR

First published 1981
Australian copyright 1981
Philippine copyright 1981
This edition 1981

© Mary Wibberley 1981

ISBN 0 263 73602 4

Set in Monophoto Baskerville 11 on 11 pt.

Made and printed in Great Britain by Richard Clay (The Chaucer Press) Ltd, Bungay, Suffolk

CHAPTER ONE

JANNA felt sorry for the man. She didn't know why she should, he looked no different from the other dozen or so patrons of the bar, except that perhaps he was sober. But he looked tired and hungry, and he looked as though he didn't have much money. The faded tartan shirt and jeans that he wore were patched and well worn. Two days' growth of beard did nothing to improve his disreputable appearance, and he had walked in as though he wanted nothing more than a quiet meal, in peace.

She went over to the table he had chosen in the corner nearest the door.

'Señor?' she asked.

He looked up from the cigarette he was hand-rolling. His eyes were bleak and hard, a darker grey than her own. The part of his face that wasn't covered by stubbly black beard was deeply tanned, and his nose was aquiline, his mouth wide.

'Coffee, please—black,' he answered in rapid Spanish, 'and food. What have you, boy?'

He looked as though he needed a double portion of everything. Janna smiled at him, just a little smile. She was used to being called boy now—She had cut her beautiful long dark hair to ensure that the disguise was complete, and the scuffed leather trousers and shirt she wore effectively concealed any femininity—a necessary disguise in this part of the town, and only Señora Lopez knew her identity.

Only Señora Lopez, tough as a man herself, who had taken her in and given her shelter these five weeks past, to repay an old debt to Janna's father.

'The best we have, *señor*, is fish.' She lowered her voice. 'I don't recommend the meat tonight.' Her Spanish was as fluent as his. He nodded wryly, as if in appreciation of her honesty.

'Then fish it is—and plenty of vegetables.'

'*Si, señor.*'

She took him the coffee first, strong and black. The place was filling now, and it was Friday. The smell of cheap wine was strong in the room. Señora Lopez and Carlos were busy dispensing it as fast as they could, and the atmosphere was thick with cheap cigar smoke and drunken laughter. Soon she would escape to her tiny room at the back, before the bottles started flying. Señora Lopez could cope, but she preferred Janna out of the way when the tough mob came in from the oil refinery a mile or so away at the docks.

Janna pulled a face as she slid the fish from the pan and ladled on a heap of beans and potatoes. The stranger wouldn't know she was giving him extra, nor would Señora Lopez, if she carried the tray so that it was out of sight from the bar.

'*Señor?*' She slid the plate in front of him. 'Wine with your meal?' He shook his head, looked at the plate, then at her, and something that might have been the beginning of a smile showed on his face as he spoke.

'No, thanks. Do you always give such large portions here?'

Janna looked round briefly to make sure Señora Lopez hadn't heard. She hadn't. She was arguing with a tough-looking man, a seaman from one of the boats in dock. He had been in before, and was always drunk.

'You looked hungry, *señor*,' she said. Her voice was naturally husky, and she had learned to deepen it slightly in the last few weeks, and keep her face slightly dirty when she worked, and no one ever looked at her twice. She was Señora Lopez' nephew to anyone who asked—and they didn't ask again, for fear of the Señora's displeasure . . .

'I am. *Gracias*.' He nodded briefly in dismissal. Janna hesitated. He could probably look after himself, but——

'*Señor*, a word of advice.' She had half turned away. He looked up, fork poised over plate.

'Yes?'

'When you have eaten—this place sometimes, on an evening——' She hesitated. Raised voices from the bar area were already getting quarrelsome. The locals resented the oil men, and the oil men made no attempt to hide their contempt of the locals—and the result was usually a fist fight, or worse, knives and bottles flashing.

'Gets busy?' he finished drily. 'Thanks for the warning. I'll eat and go. And you? Don't you mind?'

Janna shrugged. 'I keep out of the way, *señor*.'

'Very wise.' He looked at her slender boyish figure, and nodded.

She turned away, and, catching an impatient signal from Señora Lopez, went to serve three drunken locals with more wine. She didn't earn much, but she saved it all, and with the little money her father had left she would be able to go on in another few months and take the train to San Rafael, and from there, with any luck, get a job on a boat to

England. Every cent helped. She didn't expect a tip from the stranger. She had been generous because he looked like the sort of lame dog her father would have helped, and frequently did. It was one reason why he had been virtually penniless when he died. Lame dogs rarely had any money.

She turned a deaf ear to the language at the table where the three locals sat. They didn't modify it for her—because they didn't know she was a woman. If they had their behaviour would have been totally different. She shuddered; it was far better this way. . . .

She was busy for the next quarter hour or so, and when she looked over at the stranger, he was finishing his meal. She darted across.

'Anything else, *señor*?'

He shook his head. 'You gave me ample. How much?' She told him, and he raised a disbelieving eyebrow. 'So little? Your profits must be small——'

Crash! A table overturned, a man's voice shouted something, and the stranger half rose, in the act of getting notes from his pocket. Janna looked at him quickly. 'It is better you go,' she said. There was a roar behind them as Señora Lopez and Carlos waded in with broom handles flying. Three men were struggling in a heap on the floor, and more were about to join in—crash! A row of bottles went flying from the bar, and Janna turned pale.

'Quickly, *señor*,' she said. 'It's getting——' A body thudded into her from behind, and she staggered sideways and fell. The next moment the man had lifted her, lashed out with his fist at the local man who had staggered into her and sent him flying back towards his comrades.

'Are you all right?' he asked. Janna, still shaken, managed to nod.

'Yes. Go—don't join in,' she whispered, and pushed him.

'What about you? You're too young for this kind of roughhouse——'

'No, I'll go to the back.' She saw the stranger's eyes narrow a split second before he pushed her aside, and as she instinctively dodged, heard him say:

'Oh no, you don't!' Fist met chin, then the place erupted as the stranger waded into the three men who had come for him. Janna clung to the pillar, hand to mouth, unable to move, trapped by a fallen table. Señora Lopez was screaming something in the background, and the whole room was a mass of bodies, fighting, swearing, shouting.

Confused, dazed, Janna felt her arm being grabbed, and nearly fell. The next moment she and the stranger were outside on the street, and running, he with his hand round her wrist.

When they turned the corner he stopped, and released her. He grinned down at her and began to laugh. 'You were right, sonny,' he said. 'That's some place you've got!'

Janna leaned against a shop door, shaking, dazed. You—you knocked them out!' she gasped. 'Three——'

'You spoke English!' he cut in, and she realised she had—she also realised, a second later, that he had too. They stared at each other.

'You're *English*?' she gasped. 'But you speak like a native!'

'So do you,' he said. 'What the hell's an English boy doing here?'

She was a boy; she must remember that. She was *not* a girl. This man might be English—but he looked like a tramp, or a hippy—or worse. She could trust no one. For the moment, it seemed, she could trust him, but she would have to go back to the café when it had all cooled down.

'It's a long story,' she said, remembering, belatedly, to pitch her voice lower. 'I used to live about twenty miles away with my father, but he died recently. Señora Lopez gave me a job. When I've enough saved I'm going to get a boat to England.'

He gave a low whistle, then he fished several notes from his pocket and put them in her hand. 'I never paid for my meal,' he said with a faint grin showing on his face. 'There's extra for you. Save it, kid. And keep out of fights, you're not big enough yet.' He half turned, as if to go, and Janna saw a battered Land Rover parked by the wall. A ragged street urchin loitered by it, and he beckoned the boy over, fished half a note from his shirt pocket, and handed it to him. The boy, with a huge grin and a *'Gracias, señor'* matched it up with another piece from his pocket and vanished swiftly into the night. Janna smiled to herself. An old trick—especially in the rougher parts of South American cities—which ensured a car being looked after by the toughest street arab around. The man had sense, apparently—and slightly more money than she had imagined. The wad of notes in her hand was, by touch, far more than the meal justified.

'Thanks,' she said. 'Every little helps.'

'I'll be on my way,' he said. *'Adios.* Keep your chin up—and well out of the way of flying bottles——' He hesitated. 'How old are you?'

'Sixteen,' Janna lied. At nineteen, she looked like a sixteen-year-old youth. It was the age she had agreed on with Señora Lopez. She half turned away. The man was looking at her as if puzzled. It was time to go—his eyes were too hard and shrewd, and the street was ill-lit. 'Goodbye.'

'Wait,' he said. His voice was as hard as his eyes. 'Where are you getting a boat from? *Here?*'

She shook her head. 'No, San Rafael.'

'But that's a couple of hundred miles away.'

She nodded, and put the notes in her pocket. 'I know. These'll help.' She looked at him, nodded, was about to say goodbye again, when she caught her breath. 'Your arm—' she gasped, 'it's cut!' The sleeve of his shirt was dark and shiny in the dim light. He held it up, winced, and said a brief word that proved he hadn't guessed she was a woman. It was a totally unrepeatable epithet. 'That bastard had a knife—I thought I'd deflected it.'

'It's bad,' she said. 'Let me see.' He held his arm away as if he didn't want her to touch, and rolled the sleeve up. The gash was long, apparently deep, and the blood was welling up. 'My God,' she muttered. Her father would have known exactly what to do, being a doctor. She had learned enough from helping him over the years to know the flow must be stopped. She wore a small waist apron, and she took it off and handed it to him. 'Bind that above your elbow,' she said. 'You need a doctor.'

'No.' He shook his head. 'Thanks.' He bound the strip of cloth round. 'I've got first aid equipment in my Rover.'

'Let me help.' The blood had dripped on to the ground. He hesitated, then said:

'Okay, thanks.' He unlocked the door and climbed in, and Janna followed.

They found a large box and opened it, and Janna moved swiftly, selecting what was needed, lint, bandage, plaster, antiseptic liquid. She did her work deftly, and in minutes the man had a neatly bandaged arm, which he looked at, then at her. 'You're good,' he said. 'You'd make a fine doctor, better than a waiter. Your boss will go bankrupt if you give everyone double helpings!'

She laughed. 'My father *was* a doctor,' she said. 'I helped him many times. He was a damned fine one too.' She looked away and blinked hard. Tears were feminine, and she was a boy. She mustn't forget that. 'You need treatment, though, probably stitches. Why won't you go to a doctor?'

'Because.' He said it flatly.

She was treading on thin ice, she knew, but the man wasn't dangerous to her, she sensed that. His questions had shown concern. 'Are you on the run?' she asked. 'Because——' and she made a move to the pocket where she had put the money. He had probably saved her life, certainly saved her from injury.

'Let's say I'd rather not get anyone too interested in me,' he answered dryly and added, 'Keep that, I don't need money.'

Passers by looked at the Land Rover, faces sickly yellow in the dim light. Janna never went out after dark. At least the bar was a safe, well lit place—or had been safe, until minutes ago. She would go straight to the little cell she called her room, and stay there. Señora Lopez would be too busy cleaning up, in the unlikely event that anyone had called the police. José Luis Garrillo, the police chief, usually waited until trouble was over before putting in an appearance. That way guaranteed him a peaceful night with no cells to clean up the following morning. She suddenly felt weary of the sordid little town and its people. Then she remembered. . . .

'The Mission,' she said quietly. 'Of *course*! You

can go there. They'll ask no questions, and the priest is a doctor—or was.'

'Where is it?' He looked down at his arm as he spoke. The red was seeping through the bandage even though she had bound it tightly.

'About five kilometres away.'

'Can you show me?'

'Yes, only—' She hesitated. They wouldn't know her. Father Simeon had had no contact with her father. He and the priests did good work among the poor and down-and-outs of Santa Cruz, but her father kept well away. She had never known why. 'All right,' she said.

'Why the hesitation?'

'Nothing.' He might wonder why she hadn't sought shelter with them. How could she tell him? There were no women at the Mission, only three dedicated priests. 'Only my father never had anything to do with Father Simeon—so don't say who I am, will you?'

'Will they ask?'

'It's possible.'

'I don't know who you are anyway. What's your name, kid?'

'Jan Thorne—Jan's short for Jonathan,' she improvised hastily.

'Okay, Jan. My name's Lucas Tallon—called Luke.' He laughed. 'Let's go. If they ask I'll say you're my son. You could just qualify.'

She looked at him to see if he were joking, but he wasn't. A reluctant smile grew on her face. 'Right, Dad,' she said. 'Down here, left at the end.'

'Then I'll drop you back at your place,' he said. 'Thanks for coming.' He started the engine and drove down the dusty dirt track that passed for a main road.

They bumped along, and the lights of the town were left behind, and Janna held on to the dashboard, feet braced. Above the roar of the engine, Luke Tallon shouted: 'How far now?'

'Two—three kilometres. Straight along, past these trees.' The landscape was bleak, trees few and far between as yet, several miles before dense jungle took over. There, on the borders between civilisation and the primitive Indian tribes, was a kind of no-man's-land, a borderland. Janna had been along it many times with her father on his visits to a tribe of Indians who lived by the banks of the Rio Verde. She had helped to deliver an Indian baby when the mother might have died without attention.

They had treated John Thorne like a king after that. She smiled to herself. She could have taken shelter with them. Primitive and savage though they were, they had a code for living that surpassed that of the inhabitants of the town they had just left.

The air was cold and she shivered slightly, and Luke Tallon reached into the back, without taking his eyes off the road ahead, and threw a sleeveless sheepskin jacket on to her lap. 'Put that on,' he said.

'Thanks.' She eased herself into it. It was miles too large, but what a marvellous camouflage it provided.

'You're too skinny,' he observed. 'You're in a tough world, Jan. You're too young to be on your own.'

'I manage,' she said, and he looked at her briefly, but didn't answer.

'Know any judo or karate?' he asked, after a few minutes.

'No.' She swallowed. 'Do you?'

He laughed. 'Yes. If we had more time I'd teach you some.'

'We're nearly there. See the church?'

'Yes.'

'Drive in at this side.'

'Okay.' He swung the Land Rover wheel to the right and they bumped to a halt outside a long white building behind the small, primitive church. A man clad in grey woollen habit came out from an open doorway, light spilling out with him in a golden glow.

He greeted them in Spanish, and Luke answered, telling them that he and his son were travellers, that he had been injured in a bar, that someone had suggested they seek medical advice at the mission.

'Of course, of course,' the man said.

'*Habla Ingles?*' Luke asked, and the man smiled.

'Yes. You are English?'

'Yes.'

'Ah, good. I like nothing better than a chance to practise my English—it's getting rusty.' The priest had an American accent. 'You are both very welcome. Come in and I will ask Father Simeon to see you. Have you eaten?'

'Yes, thanks.' The priest ushered them into a warmly lit room, practically bare of furniture and with rough adobe walls, but the atmosphere was one of peace and quiet.

'Sit down, my sons.' The priest was tall and gaunt, almost totally bald, and possibly in his sixties. But his face was kindly, and he produced a stone flagon and three rough beakers and poured a coarse red wine out.

Luke and Jan sat at the scrubbed wooden table. They were obviously in a kitchen. There was a primitive cooker, a sink, and rows of shelves with plates and vegetables on. Luke looked at her and grinned. His arm was bleeding profusely, but it

didn't seem to bother him. He nursed it against him
and sipped the wine. The priest looked at it. 'That's
not very nice,' he remarked. 'I'm not going to pry—
we don't do that here—but it would help Father
Simeon if he knew what kind of wound it was.'

'A knife. I—er—didn't move fast enough,' Luke
answered wryly.

The priest shook his head. 'I'll go and get him in
a minute, he's in the church at the moment.'

'Don't disturb him,' said Luke. 'This can wait.'
He held up his beaker. 'Cheers, Father. Thank you
for your hospitality.'

'Cheers,' the priest answered. 'And it's Brother
Marcos.'

'Luke Tallon. My—son Jan, short for Jonathan,'
Luke answered blandly, and Janna bit her lip. The
wine was dry and harsh, but warming. She hadn't
eaten since before noon, and was now feeling
hungry.

'Brother Marcos,' she said, 'have you any bread,
please?' She gave Luke a brief look. 'My father had
eaten, but I was only beginning my meal when
the—er—trouble started.'

'Of course, of course!' The priest vanished, to
return with a bowl of yellowy butter. He produced a
loaf of coarse black bread from a cupboard and cut
her two big chunks. 'Goat butter, my son, strong but
good. Help yourself.'

'Thanks.' Janna buttered the bread and took a
huge bite. It was delicious, strong-tasting, almost a
meal in itself. Luke watched her, amused. The priest
said:

'I will go and see——' and vanished. He walked
with light, firm strides.

'Sorry, Jan, I never thought you might be

hungry. When did you last eat? You're demolishing that like it was yesterday.'

'Breakfast,' she said, between bites. 'I was busy scrubbing floors after that——' a wry smile, 'ready for the sailors to ruin tonight.'

'Tough life.' He shook his head. 'Look, it's none of my business, but do you have to go back there?'

'I don't have much choice,' she answered. 'I've no money—or not enough, yet. Señora Lopez has been good to me, after her fashion——' She shrugged. 'That's it.'

'You can go with me for a way. I'll be landing up at San Rafael—after I've done a small job.' There was hesitation in his voice, and she sensed his reluctance. He wouldn't, couldn't, be told her secret. How could she tell him? If she left with him she would have to—or would she? They were in a brightly lit room, and nothing showed on his face save polite concern. He was not looking at her remotely as a man looks at a woman. Could she carry it off? It would be the answer to her prayers if so.

'I'd be very grateful,' she said, looking not at him, but at the loaf. Dared she ask for another slice? 'But you don't want encumbering with a—boy.'

He laughed. 'Believe it or not, I feel responsible for you. Hell! If I went off and left you in that flea-hole, I'd have you on my conscience for ages.'

Janna laughed as well, more in relief than anything. She *could* manage—if he let her wear the jacket. It was odd, but it gave her a sense of anonymity. He was treating her like a child, like the youth she pretended to be. But more important, she had watched him since entering the Mission. He was no roughneck tramp, coarse and lewd, like those she met every day at the bar. He had manners, and he had spoken to the priest in a deferential manner, with the respect due to his calling. The way in which he had acted when the fight had started was another indication. He could have got out. He had been near enough to the door to escape, and he could move fast—but he had stayed because she would have got hurt if he hadn't. He possessed the chivalrous instincts of the strong to protect the weak. And because of that he had an injured arm.

'You're very kind,' she said. 'And I'd like to accept your offer. There's only one thing. I've some clothes at the place, and a box of personal possessions——'

'No trouble. When we're through here, we'll go back. Tell the good Señora you've a chance of a lift. Don't say who with.'

'She won't care, anyway,' said Janna. 'I sense she doesn't really need me there. She owed my dad a favour——'

He put up his hand to beckon her to silence as padding footsteps were heard, and Brother Marcos returned with a short round roly-poly of a man dressed in long black robes.

Luke stood up, and as he did, so did Janna. He held out his hand. 'Father Simeon? It's kind of you to see me.'

'Sit down, my son.' The priest looked at Luke's arm and shook his head. 'Tut, tut—when will men learn that fighting is not the way to achieve anything?'

Luke gave a wry grin. 'I'm sorry, Father, you're right, it doesn't. I'll try to remember that in future.' No excuse, no justification. He could have said, I got injured because I saved a stranger, but he didn't. Father Simeon gave him a very shrewd, far-seeing look, and grunted.

'Well, let's have a look at you, eh?' A thick cloth was produced by Brother Marcos and laid on the table with a black bag, and Janna watched as the elderly priest cleaned the long gash and told Luke that it needed stitching. Luke nodded. 'I thought it might. Will you?'

'I have no anaesthetic, my son. I would suggest a shot of whisky or cognac, but alas, all we have is wine.'

Luke turned to Janna. 'Jan—back of the Land Rover in a wooden box, two bottles of brandy.' He threw her the keys, and she ran out.

When she returned with them he handed one to Father Simeon. 'I hope you won't be offended by this offering, Father?' he asked. Father Simeon beamed broadly, and the cognac vanished into a cupboard. Janna poured Luke a good measure, which he drank.

'Ready when you are,' he said. Father Simeon nodded towards Brother Marcos, who stepped behind Luke.

'Young man,' he said to Janna, 'hold your father's right hand—and hold it tight, you understand?'

She nodded. 'Yes, Father.' For just a moment she hesitated. Suppose—suppose he guessed? Her hands were rough with scrubbing floors, but they weren't masculine hands. Taking a quicker breath and uttering a little prayer, she held Luke's hand tightly in both of hers and rested them on the table.

The elderly priest worked quickly and he worked well. Janna was used to seeing her father stitch patients up, and could admire the neat workmanship of this man. Luke sat unmoving, only the sweat beading his face, and the whiteness betraying the pain he must be feeling. She felt the muscles tighten in his arm, and held on grimly, as Brother Marcos held on to his shoulders. Luke closed his eyes, and his face was drenched with sweat now, but he made not a sound.

Then it was over. Father Simeon bandaged his arm and stepped back. Janna felt Luke's muscles relax, and he let out a deep sigh, more a groan than anything else, and sagged against the table. 'Thanks,' he managed to say.

Silently Janna handed him the beaker with more brandy in. He drank it in one, then looked up, and smiled. 'That's better.'

'You must stay here tonight, my sons,' said Father Simeon. 'Tomorrow I will see if you are fit to leave. There is a guest room—little more than a cell, I'm afraid—but you will be warm and comfortable.'

Luke gave a wry grin. 'That sounds fine, Father.' He looked at Janna. 'We'll do that errand tomorrow.'

'Yes, of course.' He meant her possessions. But they occupied only a small part of her mind. It was implicit that they would share a room. How on earth could she do that? Her mind went numb with a kind of horror.

'Brother Marcos will take you there—while I, with your permission, will allow myself a teeny drop of your excellent medicine.' He looked gently at the bottle, which Luke picked up and handed to him. 'With my compliments, sir.'

'Bless you, my son.' Father Simeon nodded graciously. 'Sleep well, both of you, until the morning, then.' He poured himself a very small drop of the cognac and gave them both the benefit of a warm smile.

Brother Marcos led them along a stone passage,

and opened a door, to reveal a small bare room
with two camp beds and one chair. There was one
small window high up on the wall, a candle and a
crucifix facing the door. 'The bathroom is next
door,' he said. 'Not quite up to Hilton standards,
but it will suffice, I am sure. Goodnight, my children.' He went out, closing the door quietly
behind him.

Janna and Luke were alone. Oh God, she
thought. Three hours ago he was a customer I felt
sorry for. Now I'm sleeping with him. And what's
more, he thinks I'm a boy. But for how much
longer? She took a deep breath. She had to tell
him—and the sooner the better. 'Luke,' she said,
'there's something I have to tell you.'

CHAPTER TWO

LUKE looked round. He held his arm stiffly, and he
was clearly in some pain. 'I know,' he said. 'I said
we'd get your stuff, but we can't tonight. They think
you're my son, remember? And they'd wonder what
the hell we were doing. Sorry, kid—I don't honestly
think I could drive at this moment anyway—this
arm's giving me a bit of trouble.' It was an understatement; his face was white under the tan. Janna
sat down on one camp bed.

'I'll make your bed up,' she said. 'Do you mind if
I keep your jacket on tonight? It's rather cold.'

'Sure you can—son.' He grinned. 'I'm off to the
bathroom. I'll be back.' He went out. Janna picked
up the two blankets on the camp bed and laid them
neatly over. There was one thin pillow to each bed,

covered in unbleached cotton and smelling of car-
bolic soap. Everything was spartan to say the least,
but very clean. She made up the second bed and
waited for Luke to return. She had no choice but to
stay, and accept the situation. She wouldn't tell him
now. And if this first hurdle, one night, passed well,
it might be possible. . . . But one mustn't think
ahead. Not too far.

Luke came back in, face freshly wet with water,
and shook himself like a dog. 'God, that's better,' he
said. 'I was dripping sweat.' He kicked off his shoes,
under the bed, lifted the blankets aside and lowered
himself cautiously on to his right side, careful not to
bang his arm.

' 'Night, kid,' he said. 'If I snore, don't throw
anything, just whistle—that'll stop me.'

'Goodnight. I hope your arm's better in the
morning,' she said.

'It will be.' He closed his eyes, and Janna went
out. When she returned he was asleep. She climbed
into the bed and covered herself. For some minutes
she lay there, listening to his even breathing, and
gradually relaxed. The nightmare thought, that he
might casually strip off his clothes, had been un-
necessary. She closed her eyes, leaving the one flick-
ering candle to burn in its sconce on the wall. It was
nearly at its end, and, minutes later, it sputtered
and flared briefly before going out. The room was in
pitch darkness, and all was silent outside. Gradually
she grew warmer, and then she too fell asleep.

She was awoken by a distant bell ringing, and
opened her eyes. The thin early morning light crept
tentatively into the cell, and she could just make out
the shape of Luke under his blankets in the other
bed. It couldn't be much after six. She lay there,
half dozing, half dreaming, and must have fallen

asleep again, for the next thing she knew, she was being shaken by the arm, and Luke was bending over her.

'Hey, wake up!' he said, and she opened her eyes, alarmed for one second in case he knew. 'It's only me.' He grinned down at her. 'Not the bogey-man—although I must admit I look like one. I need a shave, I'm going out to the Rover, okay? It's eight, by the way, time we were up and about.'

'Thanks, Luke.' She remembered, just in time, to pitch her voice low. He padded out and she put on her flat sandals and went to the bathroom, which was primitive in the extreme. She longed for a good wash, but it would have to wait.

She folded the blankets neatly and waited for his return. She heard the bathroom door close and ventured out to the kitchen, to find Brother Marcos clearing the table.

'Good morning,' she greeted him.

'Good morning, Jan. Did you sleep well?'

'Yes, fine, thanks.' He nodded.

'Good. I'm afraid we eat very simply here, my son. Would fish and bread suffice?'

'It sounds wonderful. Can I do it?'

'No, sit down. Everything is ready.' There was indeed a delicious aroma of food, and Janna's stomach protested. She sat down obediently and Brother Marcos placed a cup of black steaming coffee in front of her.

'Drink, I will go and get the butter for your bread. We haven't such luxuries as fridges here, but we manage, with one cold store.' He vanished, humming something vaguely Christmassy, and Janna sipped the hot sweet coffee. And a stranger walked in. At least, he looked like a stranger—until she recognised the shirt and jeans. Janna looked at

Luke, and for one moment she experienced such a shock that she nearly dropped her coffee mug. She felt her temples pound at the sight of him. Gone the rough tramp, the man for whom she had felt sorry. She was looking at an attractive stranger, dark, virile, smooth-shaven, with a wide well-shaped sensuous mouth, strong square chin, straight nose, dark grey eyes, clean black hair, shaggy and overlong, but neatly combed.

He laughed at her shock—he didn't know what kind of shock it had been, nor that her pulses pounded, because he wouldn't know *that*.

'It's me,' he said drily, and stroked his jaw. 'God, I needed that!'

'Sit down,' she said. 'You look—much better.'

'You don't need to, do you?' He peered closely at her, and she wondered if she was going red, and turned away.

'Need to what?' she asked faintly, praying for Brother Marcos's return, pretending she was looking for him.

'Shave. You will, *son*—you will.'

I won't, Dad, I won't, she thought, but wisely refrained from saying so. 'No, not yet,' she answered. 'We're having fish for breakfast.'

The priest came back in, looked at Luke, and did a double-take. 'Good heavens!' he exclaimed appropriately enough. 'You're a different man, Mr Tallon.'

'Better, I hope?' Luke asked. 'I thought it only polite.'

'Yes, indeed. A big improvement. And your arm?'

'Much better, thanks.' He stretched it out and tried, experimentally, to bend it, and winced. 'Ouch! Well, quite better.' He clenched a fist a few times, frowning, and Brother Marcos clattered

plates and produced a flat oven dish from the anci-
ent cooker upon which two succulent pieces of fish
steamed gently. The aroma of herbs teased Janna's
nostrils. Someone around here knew about cooking.

'Jan, please cut and butter the bread,' the priest
asked her. 'I think your father would find it difficult,
so do enough for him as well.' Janna nodded and
began to do so. She felt wicked about deceiving the
two kindly priests, but she had no alternative.

She still wore the old sheepskin jacket. She was,
she thought wryly, getting quite attached to it.
'Father Simeon is attending to our patients with
Brother Michel,' said Brother Marcos as he put the
plates in front of them. 'He will be an hour or so
more, I'm afraid. There's not much in the way of
entertainment here—' he gave a smile at his little
joke—'but I do have some old National Geogra-
phical Magazines you might care to look at.'

'That's kind of you, Brother Marcos, but as a
matter of fact we have to go into Santa Cruz to get
some provisions. We'll just have time if we leave
after we've eaten. We'll be back in less than an
hour.'

'As you wish, of course. Enjoy your food, my
sons.' He went out and left them.

'Can you manage?' Janna asked Luke.

He nodded, 'Yes.' He ate one-handed, his left
arm resting near his plate to steady it.

'You'll never drive,' she said, dismayed.

'Won't I? Watch me!' He regarded her coolly.
'Don't worry, we'll get your stuff.'

'I wasn't thinking about *that*,' she answered, an-
noyed. 'I was thinking about how you'll manage for
the next few days until your arm heals.'

'I'll have you to help, won't I?' he responded
drily.

'Yes,' she said, 'of course.'

'Do you drive?'

'I have. My dad had an old Austin. But I'm not sure I could manage a big thing like that Land Rover.'

'You will, if you have to.' He looked at her steadily. 'I'll toughen you up, lad. You'll be better equipped for getting a job back in England when I've finished with you.'

She laughed. 'Teach me judo? Like you are now?'

'Don't kid yourself,' he retorted equably. 'And wipe that disbelieving smile off your face, *son*,' the last word with irony. 'I'm still more than a match for you.'

That was a fact! It would have been almost funny at any other time—but not now. Janna sobered. 'I'm sorry, I didn't mean to be cheeky—*Dad*,' she said, and he grinned.

'Instant parenthood! I could get used to it.'

'How old are you?' she asked.

'Thirty-five. So you see, I could be your father.' If I was sixteen you could, she thought. But I'm nearly twenty, only you'll never know that. She found him a disturbing man, in so many ways, disturbing because very virile, and extending an aura of masculinity that made her feel helpless and unsure. It made her deception doubly difficult, and it hadn't been easy to begin with. She looked down at her plate and resumed eating.

'This fish is good,' she said.

'It is,' he agreed. 'Tell me, why are you nervous?'

Oh God, she prayed, don't let me make a fool of myself. Not now. How would a youth of sixteen answer?

She took a deep breath, and looked up. 'Nervous?

What the hell do you mean? *I'm* not nervous.'

'You look it.'

'It's your imagination,' she answered flatly. That was it: a touch of aggressiveness, of sureness. Not too much, though. She didn't want to find herself flying through the air from a hefty punch at any time in the future, and Luke looked as though he had quite a temper on him, *and* he thought she was a young man.

'That's more like it,' he said. 'That's better.'

'Thanks a lot, *Dad*,' she retorted, and he laughed.

'Lippy, aren't you?' he drawled. 'You're learning. You wouldn't have lasted long in that place where you were. Do you know something? For one second, yesterday, when you came across for my order, I thought it was a girl.' He grinned apologetically. 'A trick of the light.'

Janna didn't know how she kept her face calm and expressionless. Then, knowing she had to, she flared up.

'You're damned insulting,' she said aggressively, 'if you weren't handicapped I'd show you whether I was or not!'

Luke put up his arm as if to defend himself from a blow, and he was trying not to laugh. 'Sorry,' he said.

She stood up and carried her plate to the bowl, remembering to walk in a masculine way—which was difficult, but she'd had a few weeks to practise. 'Finished yet?' she asked him. 'There's coffee on the stove—want some?'

'Yes, and yes,' he answered. She took his plate from him, straight-faced, then poured out hot black coffee and put it in front of him. He produced a packet of cigarettes from his pocket. 'Want one?'

'No, thanks, I don't.' She watched him shake one out and light it. 'You were rolling your own yesterday,' she accused.

'I know. Good for the image—and the disguise.'

'You are on the run,' she said.

'No, I'm not,' he smiled thinly. 'But I don't draw too much attention to myself.'

'Hah! You didn't do so badly,' she retorted, 'knocking three men out!'

'Which is why you'll go in alone for your stuff,' he said. 'I'll keep well out of the way. Go in, tell the good Señora you've found transport—and vamos.'

'I will,' she promised.

'Then wash the plates, shout and tell Brother Marcos, and let's get going.' Luke stood up.

She put the plates in the bowl of water, scrubbed at them with the little brush, and left them to drain. As she finished the tall priest returned, walking quickly.

'Oh, good, you've not left. Would you be kind enough to take me with you into town? I have a few odds and ends to fetch back, and our only transport is a mule.'

'We'll get whatever you want,' said Luke, with a look at Janna.

'No, no, I wouldn't trouble you. Father Simeon is still busy—and besides, I like a trip to town.' He grinned disarmingly at them both.

'Okay, let's go, Jan—you sit in the back.'

The priest talked non-stop on the journey, telling them of the life at the Mission, the patients who came from far and wide, and, even as they drove along, small groups were walking back from the Mission, mothers with children, older men, and farther on a woman struggling to carry a baby while a child walked beside her, barefoot and filthy. Luke

slowed down, and Brother Marcos looked at him.
'You're going to give them a lift?' he enquired
gently.

'If they want it. She doesn't look more than a girl
herself.'

'They'll probably be covered in lice.'

Luke grinned. 'Then we'll have a wash after.'
Brother Marcos opened his door and spoke to the
woman—her young face thin and lined. Then he
clambered in the back next to Janna and the girl got
in with her children, thanking Luke in rapid Spanish.

They dropped her off at a hovel outside the town.
Janna didn't quite see what happened, but as Luke
leaned over to hand her older child to her, it seemed
as though she took something else from him. Her,
'*Gracias, señor*', was an astonished one.

Luke drove on, and the buildings lay ahead,
rough plastered walls, wooden frame houses, goats
wandering out from a yard. 'So,' remarked Brother
Marcos quietly, 'you are also a generous man.'

Luke grinned in the mirror. 'You see too much,
Brother.'

Brother Marcos laughed. 'Perhaps I do,' he
answered. 'If you'll drop me at this store, please,
and tell me where I'm to see you——'

They weren't far from Señora Lopez' bar. Luke
looked at Janna. 'We need some food as well,' he
said, and fished in his pocket. 'Get tinned stuff if you
can, and some fresh fruit and vegetables.'

'Okay.' Janna took the money from him. There
was no way she could pay him back, but she would
get his address in England when they parted, and
one day she would.

'I'll park around that corner.' He pointed to a
dirty side street; washing hung out across it, and

children played in the dust, and a few scraggy hens
pecked at the ground. Janna scrambled out after the
priest and crossed the road. A few cars were parked
outside the town's only hotel, a scabrous wooden
edifice that hadn't seen paint for years, and a few
men sat outside it on the verandah smoking and
playing cards and laughing.

They entered the store, which sold practically
everything from food to hardware to clothes. It
smelt of meat, and fish, and bad cheese. Janna
wrinkled her nose.

'Tell me,' said Brother Marcos very quietly, as
they wandered round helping themselves and taking
what they had chosen to the wooden counter where
the proprietor smiled toothlessly at them, 'why are
you pretending to be a boy?'

Janna stopped dead in her tracks, nearly dropping three tins of corned beef. She felt the blood
drain from her face. 'You know?' she whispered.

He smiled. 'Oh yes, I've been in the world a long
time, my child. Does Luke know?'

'No.' She looked at him. 'We—only met yesterday. You also guessed that we're not related?' He
nodded. 'I'm glad you know,' she said. 'You've been
so kind—I didn't like deceiving you.'

'Would you like to tell me why?' he asked
gently.

Janna went to the counter and placed the tins on
it, then walked back to where he waited, fingering
an array of garishly coloured towels. 'Please, don't
tell him,' she begged.

'You have my word.'

She told him everything. She told him about
living with her father, and her reason for working at
Señora Lopez' bar, and exactly what had happened

the previous evening, and when she had finished she said, 'And that's the full story, Brother Marcos.'

'My dear child, you should have come to the Mission.' His face was troubled. 'We would not have turned you away.'

'But I couldn't have stayed, could I?' she said gently. 'I'm nineteen—I want very much to go to England, and, if possible, trace any family I might have.'

'Do you know of any?'

'No, but my father was a doctor. There'll be registers. I can start somewhere——'

'My dear girl, have you never wondered why he came here all those years ago? He could have changed his name.'

She looked at him, shocked at hearing something she had only sensed before. He went on: 'You say your mother died giving birth to you?'

'Yes, so I never knew her. He brought me up with the help of an Indian woman—she died two years ago.'

'I see.' His face was very gentle. 'I wish you luck in your search—but I want you to promise me something. I want you to promise that you will call at an address in England. I have friends near London, very old and dear friends. We keep in touch, and they are good people. I will give you their address when we return to the Mission. They will find a way of letting me know you are safe, and they will help you.'

'I promise.' Janna was touched by his obvious concern. It warmed her and made her feel safe.

'Good. I presume you are continuing to deceive Luke for a good reason? It is not an easy thing to do, you know, live a lie.'

'I know—I'm already finding that. But it's best, don't you see?'

'Not all men are lustful brutes, my child.' He smiled gently.

'I'm sure he isn't—but, please, he might not take me if——' She stopped, biting her lip. 'I desperately want to go to San Rafael, and this is my chance.'

'I won't tell him.' He patted her arm. 'Come, let's finish our shopping. The good proprietor is looking anxious.'

Janna carried a boxful of groceries back to where Luke waited, leaving Brother Marcos talking to an elderly village woman. Then she went to see Señora Lopez, to thank her, and collect her meagre possessions. As Janna had guessed, the woman wasn't really sorry to see her go. She had seen her with Brother Marcos leaving the store, and assumed that he was connected with her departure. Janna didn't disillusion her. She took her small tin box and locked it in the cracked leather suitcase with her clothes, thanked the woman, and left. It was as if a chapter of her life had ended. She wondered what the next would hold.

It was noon, and Janna prepared a meal for the four men at the Mission, then listened to them talking outside in the shelter of the tree. She had insisted on being allowed to do this, and she was a good cook. Luke, after all, had paid for their hospitality with two bottles of brandy. She had no money to spare, or goods, so she set out to prepare a meal fit for a feast. Their laughter drifted in, the laughter of four men at ease with the world. She had locked herself in the primitive bathroom on their return, stripped and bathed, then washed her clothes, which hung out to dry. Her pants were dark blue, and could easily be a man's, but she had concealed them with a shirt, to be safe. They were already dry, minutes after being put out. She now wore a loose blue shirt and her trousers. It was too hot to wear the jacket—and it would have looked odd anyway, so she had left that on her case in the room they had occupied.

The onions and tomatoes sizzled gently in the skillet, together with the mushrooms. The rice was nearly done, and she added chilli and herbs to the aromatic mixture of meat in the other pan, and stirred. Her mouth watered, and she tasted the meat, and nodded. Five minutes more. . . .

'Jan?' It was Brother Marcos, who had walked in quietly and stood inside the door. 'Have you a moment?'

'Yes, of course,' she turned.

He handed her a piece of paper. 'This is the address of my friends. Keep it carefully—memorise it if you can, in case you lose it, and don't forget, you have promised.'

'Thank you.' She took it, read it, and committed it to memory, then folded it carefully and put it in her trouser pocket. 'I promise.'

He took something from a pocket in his robe. It was a small wooden crucifix, on a thin leather thong. 'Come here, my child,' he said, and as she moved forward, he put it round her neck. 'Wear that with my blessing,' he said, 'and may it protect you.'

Tears filled her eyes. She couldn't speak for a moment or two. 'Thank you,' she whispered at last. It went under her shirt, and was hidden. She touched it through the heavy cotton. There was something very reassuring about it. Brother Marcos smiled.

'Soon you will be on your way. His arm is healing

well. You must change the bandage for him each day for the next few days. I will pray for you every morning in the church.'

'You're very kind, Brother Marcos,' she said. 'I don't know how to thank you.'

'Do not try. Luke, I feel, is also a good man. Something is on his mind—some problem, I sense, but perhaps it is none of my business. I will pray for him as well.' His face changed. 'Now, it smells to me that our meal is nearly ready. You have worked hard. Shall I tell the others to come in?'

'Please.' Janna began to set out the plates, and he walked quietly away from her to the door. The priest was a clever man. He too realised that Luke was hiding something. She wondered what it was, and if she would ever know.

CHAPTER THREE

Two hours later Luke and Janna left the Mission and set off in the Land Rover. He drove slowly at first, as he had that morning, and soon they left civilisation behind and were climbing a rough tortuous road into the hills. Luke was very quiet, concentrating on the way, and Janna sat silently beside him. If he wanted to talk, she would, but if he didn't, she wouldn't. She was well aware that his arm must pain him, but more than that, he seemed preoccupied with something, and she knew instinctively not to interrupt his train of thought. The scenery was spectacular, dense jungle at one side, on the other a sheer drop into a valley several thousand feet

below. The road was poor, narrow in parts, with
little traffic either way. Janna was entirely in his
hands. It was a sobering thought to have. She had
no idea where they were heading. It certainly
wasn't in the direction of San Rafael, but then he had
told her he wasn't going directly there. She wondered where he was going to, and why, but she
wasn't going to ask.

She put the jacket on when the air grew cooler
with the height. Instantly she felt safer. Luke had
told her, before leaving, that she could keep it. He
had a heavier parka in the back of the Land Rover,
which was now well packed with boxes and cartons.
Some contained food, the others were closed; they
could have held anything. He had filled the Land
Rover with fuel before leaving Santa Cruz that
morning, and Janna had been surprised at the
vehicle's capacity for petrol until he had explained to
her and Brother Marcos that the Land Rover was
specially fitted with two reserve tanks. It meant that he
could travel for hundreds of miles if necessary without
stopping at a garage. It was sensible; they were few
and far between in the mountainous regions of the
Andes. Hours had passed, and they had seen no one.

Luke looked at her now as they reached a comparatively safe stretch of road. 'Don't you want to
know where we're heading?' he asked.

'No, you're the boss,' she answered.

He smiled faintly. 'Very true. But it's natural to
be curious.'

'I am. But I felt that if you wanted to tell me, you
would.'

'You must trust me,' he said lightly.

'I do.' But not enough to tell you who I am, she
thought.

'And I presume I can trust you,' he said.

'You saved me from injury—you gave me a chance to get away from there. Oh yes, you can trust me,' she answered.

It was growing darker. Night fell early here, and it was colder. She wondered where they would spend the night, and the thought sent a little shiver of apprehension down her spine. They would be truly alone, in a great wilderness of silence, and wild animals, and possible danger.

'When we stop, I'll tell you,' said Luke. 'And we'll stop soon. I don't fancy driving in darkness—not here.'

'Are we near a town?' she asked.

'Not according to the map. We'll sleep in the back here.' He nodded his head.

'Is that how you've slept?'

'Occasionally—when there was nowhere, as now.' He smiled. 'That room in the Mission was like a luxury hotel.' He switched on the powerful head-lights. 'Look out for a suitable spot.'

They drove in silence for several miles more, and it was suddenly dark, too dark to safely travel much farther. He swerved off the road, and Janna held on tightly as he bumped to a stop. They were in a clearing, not far from the road, surrounded on three sides by huge towering trees, but the ground was level.

Luke lit a cigarette, then turned out the head-lights, and the silence seemed to settle around them, and there was not another human being for miles and miles. Janna shivered. Wasn't he frightened too? Any number of nameless horrors could lurk out-side—she shook herself, chiding herself for an over-active imagination. But it was difficult to think rationally there. And what would he think of her if she put her fears into words? She didn't want his contempt. They were in darkness, the only light the glow of his cigarette.

He said suddenly: 'I'm looking for a man. I've been on his trail for weeks now, and I think I'm getting very near.'

'Who is it?' she asked.

'You wouldn't know the name if I told you. I don't intend to anyway. The less you know, the better. Tallon's not my real surname.' She felt herself going cold. Dear God, he *was* a criminal—he could be a murderer, and she was alone in this vast black wilderness with him. Helpless.

It was as if he sensed her fear, for he looked at her. She felt his movement, saw the faint blur of his face as he turned. 'It's all right,' he said, 'I can imagine what's going through your head—I can almost read your mind. You're safe, Jan. The only reason I'm travelling under another name is because he knows everyone—even the police chiefs—and my own name is a distinctive one, and I've been stopped enough times, God knows. It says on my passport that I'm a geologist, and I've got the documents to prove it. There are geological instruments in the back, and tools, and as far as anyone in South America knows, I'm just a harmless nut who goes around tapping rocks and digging and taking photographs for a book I'm writing.'

'But you're not,' she said.

'No, I'm not. The man I'm looking for has something that belongs to my father—belonged, I should say. It now belongs to me. My father died recently. Before he did, I promised I would get it back: it's as simple as that. Now you know why I didn't want to get involved in any fist fights in your café.'

'But you did,' she said. 'You could have run.'

'And let you get battered?' He stubbed out the cigarette in the ashtray. Now there was nothing at all. No light. 'You're a kid—I couldn't have—so I grabbed you and ran. I got the shock of my life when you spoke English.'

'So did I when you answered. Thanks for what you did. But won't I get in the way when you go to see—your mystery man?'

'No, I'll leave you somewhere, some town first. Don't worry, you'll get to San Rafael sooner or later. I just want you to know it might be later, but as you're in no desperate hurry——'

'But you? What about you? Aren't you going back to England too?' she asked.

'Yes. But I'll have to drive much farther. He'll be watching everything within a few hundred miles— I'll be doing a bit of smuggling, don't forget.'

'It's dangerous—I've lived here all my life, and I know that. If this man is so powerful, wouldn't you be better with someone?'

'Like you?' He laughed. 'You haven't even got a passport, have you?'

'No.' She shook her head. 'I'll have to apply for one.'

'Do you have a birth certificate?'

'Yes.'

'You won't have too much trouble then. Oh——' he paused, and she heard him tapping the dashboard.

'What?' she whispered.

'I've been thinking—just an idea at the moment. Let me think about it before I tell you. I'm going outside—stay there.' He opened his door and jumped to the ground. The door swung to, and he had disappeared, gone. Janna wondered why she

had suggested what she had. What he didn't know
was that, when the time came to leave, if he needed
her, she could tell him the truth. A man and woman
travelling together were always less suspicious than a
man alone, especially if the police were watching
out for him. She wondered what on earth he was
planning to steal back. Jewellery? Coins—the pos-
sibilities were endless. She found herself fingering
the little wooden cross. It made her remember
Brother Marcos, and she smiled to herself.

Luke got back in and reached over for his jacket.
'God, it's cold,' he muttered.

'I know.'

'Want an extra sweater on?'

'Do you have one?'

'I came prepared. Look in the back, Jan. This
damned arm's stiff. There's a case, it's not locked,
next to yours.' She leaned over and he switched on
the interior light.

A few moments later she wore a thick dark
sweater under the jacket. She was much warmer instantly. She also hoped that if they were going to
stay in high terrain for a while—and it was possible—she would be able to wear the sweater during
the day. It was figure-concealing, and therefore
comforting for her to wear. She had only to say,
look, I'm a girl—but she didn't. Luke certainly
wouldn't throw her out there and then, but he
might leave her at the first opportunity—at a Mission—simply because what he was going to do
might be dangerous. There was also a certain rap-
port building up between them. If she told him pre-
maturely, the atmosphere would undoubtedly
change. She had met very few men in her life, and
those she had had either been native Indians, or the
kind of rough, tough men who made their home in

primitive places and acted accordingly. She just didn't know what he would do, and she couldn't take a chance on it. Her father had always warned her of the kind of man she would meet, in Santa Cruz, or any larger town, had always impressed on her never to be alone—she had broken the rules simply by coming with Luke, but then her father wasn't here any more to protect her. She was on her own now, and her instincts told her she would be better, and safer, by letting Luke go on thinking she was male.

In one way her instincts were right—but in another way, she couldn't have been more wrong. Her own inexperience of men was to let her down on something she couldn't even have imagined. But fortunately for her peace of mind, she was blissfully unaware of it at that moment—and for the hours following.

'That's much better,' she said. 'I'm warmer now.'

'Want anything to eat?'

'Not particularly. Do you?'

'No. We'll wait till morning. If you're thirsty, there's a water container at the back.'

'I saw it. Shall I move things for you to sleep?'

'You can help. I've got blankets, and a sleeping bag. Only one—I'm sorry. I didn't think I'd be taking on a passenger.'

'Can I sleep on the front seat?' she asked.

'If you like. Why not?' He pressed it. 'It should do you. Okay, let's get bedded down.'

The next minutes were spent making a space for Luke at the back. He gave her two blankets, and after she had been outside she got in again and locked both doors, then lay down. She had wedged a squashed cardboard box between the seats, to make a level surface for herself, and was surprised to find her makeshift bed not at all bad.

'Goodnight, Luke,' she said.

'G'night.'

She marvelled at his ability to fall asleep. Within minutes, his breathing had changed, become deeper and steadier, while she lay awake, musing at the strangeness of it all, and how chance had led him into that bar that night, out of all the places he could have stopped at. On that rather profound thought she drifted off into sleep.

She woke early, stiff and sore from the narrow place, and climbed quietly out so as not to wake the deeply sleeping man. A thick mist, clinging, damp, and heavy, obscured everything save their immediate surroundings. Janna did a few exercises to restore her circulation before getting back in the Land Rover, and sat quietly waiting for Luke to wake up. She would have started preparing food, but all the necessary equipment was buried in the back of the vehicle. She had no idea of the time. Her father's watch that she wore had stopped, and it could have been any time from dawn to eight o'clock. She was hungry, and thirsty, but Luke needed his sleep far more than she. His was the greater task, to drive, and with an arm that must still be painful, or at least uncomfortable.

She sighed and sat back, and thought over her life, wondering if she would ever find anyone to whom she was related. Her father had never spoken about England; it was as if he had put it out of his mind when he had gone to South America. And Janna, sensing a deep hurt, had never asked. But she wanted to belong, not to be alone, as she had been these past few weeks, not belonging, unhappy, unsettled. It was very important to her to go to England——

He moved, groaned, sat up, and looked round. 'Oh,' he said, 'you're there.'

'Where did you expect me to be?' she asked.

'I just had a dream—it must have been a dream,' he told her, 'and you'd gone. God, it was a weird one too.' He scratched his head and looked blearily at her. 'I could do with a cup of coffee.'

'I didn't want to wake you. Now you are awake—if you pass me the stove I'll get it lit outside. There's a thick mist all round us.'

Luke squinted round. 'So there is. Here.' He passed her the small camping stove and she knelt over and took it from him.

'Hang on. I'll be back for water and coffee,' she said, and eased herself out. Minutes later, the water was boiling away in the billy can. She stirred in the instant coffee and filled the two tin mugs, then put the billy can on again with the contents of a can of stewed meat and vegetables to heat.

'Ugh!' he tasted the coffee and looked at her. 'I forgot we were so high up.' He sat on the step of the Land Rover.

She sipped, and pulled a face. 'It boils at a lower temperature, doesn't it?'

'It sure does. Talk about lukewarm——' He grimaced. 'It's wet, that's about all you can say.'

'I did my best,' she protested, stung by his tone.

Luke lifted one eyebrow. 'I never said you didn't,' he answered, amused.

Janna bit her lip. It was stupid to take offence at a casual comment. It was true anyway, the coffee tasted foul. She hoped the stew would be an improvement. He had only one plate, and she put hers into the empty mug and handed him the plateful. It tasted much better, hot enough to enjoy, but not too hot. They ate in silence and she cleaned plate and mug with paper tissue.

Luke stood up. 'Will you do my arm?' he asked.

'Yes. Then do we go?'

'Not until this has lifted. We'd be over the side faster than you could say knife.'

'So we wait?'

'We wait.'

'But it might be clear in a mile or so——'

'Do *you* want to drive?' he asked. 'What's the hurry, anyway?'

'No.' She shook her head. She didn't know herself.

'Well then,' he turned away and climbed in. 'Leave the stove to cool out there. Get in and shut the door. I want a cigarette and I'm damned if I can smoke out here.'

Janna scrambled in and slammed the door. She was vaguely irritated, and to make it worse, she didn't know why. She watched him light up, mouth set, and he looked at her. Voice heavy with sarcasm, he asked: 'You don't disapprove of me smoking, do you?'

'Of course not,' she said coldly, and turned away.

'You sure as hell look it,' he observed.

'I can't help how I look,' she retorted. She wanted to stop, but she couldn't.

'You *can* help your expression,' he said, 'and yours is asking for a thick lip.'

'Why don't you, then?' she snapped. 'And do your own damned bandage!'

'What the hell's the matter with you?' he demanded, steely-eyed, and, when she still obstinately turned away, grabbed her chin roughly and turned her to face him. 'And look at me when I'm speaking to you!'

'Go to hell!'

He released his hold on her abruptly. 'By God, but you're asking for it,' he grated. 'If you weren't a kid——'

She remained, lips clamped tightly together, fighting back the treacherous tears that would be a giveaway, and looked at him, defiance in every inch of her.

The atmosphere in the Land Rover was brittle with anger, and she saw his eyes, saw the visible effort he was making to control it, and she was afraid of him. The awful part was, she didn't know why it had happened. It was as if both were under a sudden strain. She had seen Luke in action, fighting off three drunken men—he was very strong, and he didn't know she was a woman, and he could quite easily lash out at her, because he was as tense as she, and for him that might be the only way he knew.

She opened the door and jumped down to the ground. 'Where the hell are you going?' he demanded.

'Nowhere—just—I won't be a minute.' She walked towards the trees. When the Land Rover was out of sight she stopped, and discovered her legs were trembling. She put her hand to her face. What did she do now? Apologise? Let him think she was a cissy, it didn't matter. She knew that if he hit her, even if he didn't intend it to be hard, he could hurt her badly. She hugged her arms to her sides and leaned against a tree. I mustn't cry, I mustn't cry, she repeated silently. Boys don't cry, not at sixteen anyway——

'Jan! Come on back!'

She heard his voice, and went back towards the

Land Rover. He stood outside it, waiting. 'I'm sorry,' she said. 'I've no right to be cheeky.'

Luke nodded. 'Okay. Are you going to change the dressing or not?'

'Yes.' She sniffed, tears safely out of sight, and followed him in. He had the first aid box ready, and she busied herself, in the limited space, setting everything to hand.

His arm, when she had unrolled the bandage that Father Simeon had put on the previous day, looked healthy enough, and she applied fresh ointment, covered the stitches with lint, and began to wind the bandage round very carefully and gently, all her concentration on not hurting him. She didn't want him angry again.

'How does that feel?' she asked at last.

'Fine, thanks.' He grinned at her—actually *grinned*. 'All right, stop looking so scared, I'm not going to punch you. I need you to look after my arm.'

She gave him a rather shaky smile in return. 'That's a relief!'

'Ever been in a scrap?' he asked.

She shrugged. 'Just a few,' she lied.

'I must teach you how to look after yourself.' He reached out and squeezed her arm above the elbow. 'God, where are your muscles?'

She jerked him away. 'That wasn't fair—my—my arm's relaxed.'

'That's why I did it. You need feeding up, sonny.'

'I'm okay,' she muttered.

'In England maybe—here, no. Definitely no. Don't worry, I'll show you a few exercises that'll develop your biceps. Ever done press-ups?'

She shook her head. She didn't know what he meant. 'No.'

'I can't show you yet, until this arm's right, but they'll do the trick.'

'You seem very concerned about my strength,' she said. He wasn't angry any more. Let him stay that way. It would make life easier, over the next few days.

'Let's say I'm concerned about a youngster in a bad land.'

'And you, of course, can look after yourself anywhere?' she remarked lightly.

'I hope so. I've been almost everywhere there is to go.'

'Are you an explorer?' she asked.

He laughed. 'No, nor a geologist. But I know enough about it to pass muster.'

'What do you do, then?'

'Do you really want to know?' He looked at her, amused.

'I wouldn't ask if I didn't,' she retorted. 'However, if I'm being too nosey, say so.'

'You're being naturally curious. You never get anywhere without asking questions in this world, Jan. I'll tell you. My grandfather founded a big chemical firm—big now, I mean. It wasn't when he began. He started off in a small back room making herbal ointments, cough medicines, stuff like that. By the time my father inherited it, it was pretty big. He worked hard, and expanded, and we've got factories all over the world now, producing life-saving drugs—but we still make those old-fashioned ointments we began with, and they still sell in chemists' shops all over the world. So in a sense, your father and mine were in the same line of work.'

He paused. 'Ever heard of—no, sorry, I'd better not tell you—yet.' He grinned.

'Charming!' Janna breathed. 'Keep me in suspense?'

'Something like that.'

'So where do you fit into this?'

'I've got two brothers. My father left control of everything between us. Mark is in England, he's one year younger than I am, and he's dedicated to the job. Bob's four years younger than me, working in Australia at that end. And me—I'm the one who travels around finding sites for new factories all over the world.'

'Oh. You like doing that?'

'I can't sit on my backside like Mark—so yes, I do. But this is different. This is another matter entirely. My father was a philatelist. He had the most fantastic collection of stamps you've ever imagined. Nine years ago, a South American character, by the name of Don Raul Cordilla, whom he knew well and trusted, tricked him out of an album of rare and precious stamps—including a Cape Triangular. Ever heard of it?'

Janna shook her head. 'No.'

'It's extremely rare and valuable. Raul Cordilla vanished, and nothing was heard of him until last year, when my father read a small item in a stamp magazine that set him on the trail again. He'd been obsessed with getting that stamp back—not particularly the others, but that one. Cordilla's a greedy man, a collector of everything rare and beautiful for his own gratification. He's also a thief. I'm going to get that stamp back from him.'

'How?'

He looked at her. 'I've got a few plans. Obviously I'm not going to march up to his front door, knock, and announce myself. Nor would I be fool enough

to try burglary—but there are ways.' He smiled
thinly. 'I don't know which plan I'll use until I see
exactly where he lives and how accessible he is. He's
also a vain man—very vain.'

'He'll know you,' Janna pointed out. 'He'll recognise you.'

'He last saw me—briefly—ten years ago, when he
was a guest at our house. I was young and brash. I
also had a beard because that was in fashion—I'm
different now, I promise you. He won't recognise me
at all.'

She digested the information for a few minutes in
silence. To her it was incomprehensible that a scrap
of paper could be worth such a lot of money—or
even worth risking a life for.

'What are you thinking?' asked Luke, as if he
sensed this.

She told him, and his face tightened. 'I made a
promise. I'm going to keep it,' he said, and his jaw
was hard and decisive.

'But—when you get it—what then? Do you *need*
the money?'

'No.' He looked at her, puzzled. 'I don't understand *you*,' he said quietly. 'It's a matter of principle,
don't you see?'

'No, I don't,' she retorted, forgetting all her previous promises to herself to keep calm. 'Nothing's
worth the risk you're going to take.' She felt angry
with him, but she didn't understand why herself.
She felt suddenly frightened for him, and the feeling
was a dismaying one. What's the matter with me?
she thought, bewildered. Why should I care about
this stranger? But she did. She didn't want him to
get hurt. The knowledge, the sudden awareness of
why, sent a wave of pain through her, and she clen-

ched her fists tightly. Dear God, don't let me give myself away, she thought.

'Then you're much different from me,' he said, and his voice held the hardness of anger. He didn't realise the truth of his words.

'So I am,' she retorted. 'Because money's not important——'

'Damn you,' he cut in, 'where the hell do you think you'd be without it? Back at that bar, slaving away to scrape enough up to get back to England——'

'Yes! And I'd have done it!' she blazed.

'Oh yes? You can't even look after yourself when a fight starts. You were paralysed with fear. How the hell would you have got to San Rafael in one piece? There are men looking for boys like you.'

Janna was shaking with a mixture of fear and anger. 'What the hell do you mean?' she gasped.

He laughed. 'God, you're stupid as well. Didn't your father teach you the facts of life, sonny?'

'Don't call me stupid. I'm not, you are!' she exclaimed, fists clenched. She wished she *were* a man. She hated him, hated the tough arrogance of him.

He gripped the wheel tightly as if he would like it to be her neck. 'I'd advise you to shut up,' he said grimly. 'You've said enough——'

'No, I haven't,' she stormed. 'And I won't shut up! Who do you think you are anyway? I should have stayed in town—or at the Mission——'

'I wish to God you had,' he grated. 'I can do without your childish tantrums. You deserve a bloody good hiding, and by God, one of these days you'll get one—and I hope I'm there to see it!'

Incensed beyond all reason, Janna lashed out at him and caught him a stinging blow on his face. She pushed the door open, jumped out, and ran towards the trees, the tears blurring her eyes, her feet like lead. It was like some awful dream where you can't escape. She heard Luke's footsteps pounding after her, and fear filled her so much that she could hardly breathe. Sobbing, panting, she crashed into a tree, blinded by her tears, and staggered back from it dazed. Luke caught her arm, swung her round and pulled her towards him. She saw the deep welling of anger on his face, the dark, hard face, and then he thrust her away from him as if she burned him.

'Get back in the Land Rover,' he ordered, as she stumbled, and scrabbled for balance. 'Before I beat the hell out of you!'

'No! I'm going—leave me——' she sobbed, incoherently. He pulled her to her feet and shook her hard, then slapped her face.

'You're not going anywhere,' he said, and pushed her in the direction of the waiting vehicle. 'You're getting in there, and then you'll apologise.'

Her mouth was swollen where he had hit her. Stumbling, nearly falling, she half ran, pushed inexorably in the direction of the Land Rover, and when she reached it she put both her hands out to stop him from pushing her in.

'No—no——!' she shouted.

Luke grasped her arm, twisted it round behind her back, and she was helpless. She fell to her knees, and he reached over to pull her up again—and as he did so, his arm brushed against her breast.

She heard, as if from a long way away, his sudden exclamation—and then: 'Oh, my God——!' in a long-drawn-out, shaky breath. The next moment he had let her go, and she saw him move away, almost as if drunk, and lean against the Land Rover, facing it, his forehead resting against the side. He had gone almost grey with shock.

Janna pulled herself painfully to her feet and put her hand to her throbbing cheek and mouth. She could no longer fight him. She felt weak and helpless. She crumpled slowly to the ground, her legs giving way, and Luke turned, equally slowly, and looked at her. He looked like a man who had received a stunning blow, white, trembling. She put her arm in front of her face as if to shield herself from further blows, as he walked slowly towards her.

'Get up,' he said.

'No.' Her mouth trembled. 'Please—don't hit me again——'

'Dear God, hit you?' he exclaimed, and his voice held horror. 'Jan, why didn't you tell me?' She saw the agony in his eyes, and then, belatedly, realised that he knew.

CHAPTER FOUR

JANNA got to her feet very cautiously, very carefully. She ached all over, but particularly on her mouth. She stood and faced him, ashen-faced, trembling, then she saw what was in his eyes, and cried helplessly.

'Why didn't you tell me?' he repeated, and the anger had gone. He looked as though he was still recovering from shock.

'I was frightened,' she whispered.

'You nearly got yourself beaten up,' he snapped. 'Don't you understand? I've never hit a woman in my life.' He put his hand to his face and rubbed it. 'Oh, God, why—why?'

'I thought it was better. I'd been pretending to be a boy when I worked at Señora Lopez' place—she thought it was wise. And when you came in, and then the fight and everything, it seemed l-logical to keep on pretending.'

Luke held out his hand. It shook with a fine tremor. 'Look at that. You don't know what you've done to me, Jan.'

'I'm sorry,' she whispered.

'Get in the Land Rover. I need a drink,' he said, and she obeyed. When they were both in he reached over and found a flask from the small compartment at the front. He offered it to her. She took it and swallowed some, and he followed suit. 'You should have told me,' he said. 'I could have nearly killed you.' He looked at her. 'I knew there was something wrong, but I never guessed what it was. I thought you were effeminate, heaven help me—I wondered what I'd got myself into. Do I have to spell it out for you? I thought that—I—was——' he seemed to be having difficulty finding the right words. 'I was beginning to think there was something wrong with *me*.' He gripped the steering wheel tightly. 'Which was why I got so bloody mad with you. You had me worried.' Some of his colour was coming back. 'Did I hurt you badly?' Janna nodded. 'Let me see.' He took hold of her chin very gently and looked at her face. 'I would never have touched you if I'd known,' he said. 'You know that, don't you?'

'Yes,' she whispered. She ran her tongue over her lips and tasted blood. Luke saw, and closed his eyes briefly.

'I'm sorry. Forgive me,' he said it very quietly.

'I'm sorry too. For getting mad at you—for getting *you* mad,' she whispered. 'I don't know why I did.'

'Is your name really Jan?'

'Janna.' She managed a faint smile.

'Janna. I'll have to get used to that, won't I?' He let out a deep sigh. 'What a mess!'

'Would you have offered me a lift if I'd told you the truth?' she asked.

He shook his head. 'I don't know. I wouldn't have left you there, that's for sure, but I might have left you at the Mission. I just don't know.'

'Do you want me to go back there?' she asked, and he looked at her.

'No, not now. But I may alter my plans. I'll have to see.' He smiled faintly. 'I can't get you involved in any danger.'

'I'm strong—for a woman,' she told him. 'And I'm not afraid.'

'I'm sure you're not.' He laughed. 'No wonder you didn't have much muscle!' He raked his fingers through his hair. 'I'm still suffering from shock,' he admitted. 'You hit me pretty hard—when I touched you, I thought for a second I was imagining things. What a fool I've been, not to have realised!' He stared at her. 'You don't even look like a boy!'

'Brother Marcos knew. He made me promise to contact some friends of his in England.' Janna fished under the sweater and shirt and pulled out the crucifix. 'He gave me this as well.'

'And I suppose you asked him not to tell me?' Luke touched the wooden cross and then let it fall. 'He's a kindly soul. I liked him. Put it away, you don't want to lose it.' He watched her do so, then added: 'Now I see why you wanted to wear my jacket.'

'And your sweater,' she added drily. 'Are you very angry with me?'

'I'm more relieved than anything at this moment. I was getting disturbing vibrations from you which I didn't understand.' He grinned faintly. 'In other words, I'm a normal male, with normal male instincts—and I was beginning to wonder what was happening to me!' She felt herself go fiery red, as she realised the implications of his words, and he added: 'You're quite safe. How old are you?'

'Nearly twenty.'

'Ever had a boy-friend?'

'No.' She shook her head, still pink.

'Then you're doubly safe. Your innocence is a great protection.' He put his hand out and held hers. 'When Father Simeon was stitching my arm, and made you hold my hand——' he smiled wryly, 'I thought then your hands were like a girl's. And the first time, in the bar, when you came over to take my order, I thought for a moment, and I think I've already told you, that you were a girl— but, stupid fool that I am, I dismissed the thoughts after. Weren't you scared, having to share a room?'

'I was terrified you'd strip off or something—and expect me to do the same,' she admitted. 'It was quite a relief when you didn't.'

Luke laughed. 'You poor kid! How on earth did you expect to keep up the charade for days?'

'I don't know. I'm glad now you've found out,' she said.

'It makes life easier in one way,' he answered, 'and in another, more difficult.' He sighed.

'Why?'

'Because you *are* a woman, that's why. This is a

difficult country for a woman—I feel responsible for you, Janna. Oh God, how can I leave you in some strange town, while I go off?'

'Let me come with you,' she begged. 'Don't you *see*? Now you know about me? A man and a woman travelling together—no one would look twice. We could pretend to be married——' She stopped. Perhaps she had gone too far.

'No, don't stop there. You might have something.' He regarded her very seriously. 'Your hair's short, but that's the fashion nowadays. You look feminine—I must have been blind not to realise—and as you say, a man and woman together——' he nodded. 'Mmm, I must think about that.'

Janna felt completely different from a mere half hour previously. A great burden had rolled away. The tension had evaporated, and Luke too was looking more his normal self. The mist, as if in sympathy with them, was lifting rapidly and a weak sun filtered through.

'I'll get the stove and we'll go,' he said. 'We might make Rio d'Oro tonight, and if we do, we'll make our plans.' He jumped down from the vehicle and went over to the camping stove.

Ten minutes later they were on their way.

They reached Rio d'Oro in the early evening. It was a teeming city, with slums and shanty houses at one end, and luxury villas at the other. In between, the whole spectrum of human nature, night clubs, bars, restaurants, hotels, and cars everywhere. The streets were brightly lit and garish, and thronged with people, and they drove down the main Avenida with its flashing neon signs and laughing pedestrians, and Janna gazed in wonder. She had never seen anywhere like it in her life. Music blared out from lighted arcades and shops, and the noise blended into a cacophony of riotous sound.

'There's an hotel near here,' said Luke, 'where we'll stay. I could do with a bath, I don't know about you.'

'Oh, luxury!' she laughed.

'We're from Santa Cruz, we're natives of South America, and we're married,' he said, and she sobered suddenly.

'What?'

He spared her a brief glance. 'Your idea, remember?'

'Yes.' She went very quiet, and he added: 'I have no designs on you—I just prefer you with me. For obvious reasons. Look around you. You've never been anywhere like this before, have you?'

'No.'

'And you don't know what the men are like. They eat little girls like you.' He smiled. 'Think of a name for us.'

'Lopez?'

'Fair enough, Lucas and Janna Lopez. Señor and Señora Lopez. Fine, here we go.' He turned off the main road, and into a quieter, less brightly lit street, down that, turned again, and they drove into the large car park of a white hotel which proclaimed itself to be: 'Hotel Negresco.'

His Spanish was perfect. Janna didn't know where he had learned it, but he spoke like a native, and within a quarter of an hour they were in a large room, with old but gracious furniture and a huge double bed. The receptionist had been dismayed at their appearance, but a casually flashed wad of notes had ensured a quick change of face, and a deferential manner.

Janna looked round the room, then at the bed, then, slowly, at Luke. He put up his hand. 'Don't say it,' he warned.

'But——'

'I know what's going through your mind. When I get into bed, I sleep. Okay? And if you think I'm offering to kip down on the floor, I'm sorry to disappoint you. My chivalry doesn't run that far.' He crossed over to her and cupped her face in his hands. 'You're safe, Janna. Don't you realise?'

She nodded, feeling such warmth and strength from the touch of his hands that she wanted to tell him. 'Yes,' she whispered.

'Good. Now, have you got anything a bit more feminine in that case of yours, or do we go out and see if there are any shops open?'

'I've got one dress,' she said. 'But I made it myself—it's nothing wonderful.'

'Let me see it.' He didn't release her immediately, but stroked her mouth with a gentle finger. 'The swelling's going down. You may have a bruise tomorrow—and I only slapped you at quarter strength. I shudder to think how you'd look if I'd belted you as hard as I was tempted to.'

'I'll buy some make-up tomorrow,' she said. 'That'll help.'

'Yes.' He let her go and turned away. 'Get your dress.'

She had it rolled up at the bottom of the case. Simple cotton, sleeveless, in blue, it was creased, but she shook it out and held it up. 'That's fine,' said Luke. 'If you're having first bath hang it up and let the steam get at it.' He kicked off his shoes and went over to the bed. 'Off you go. I'll lie down till you're through.'

They had their own bathroom, little more than a

cubicle with tiles, but the water gushed out scalding hot, and Janna wallowed in it, washed her hair as well, and emerged feeling really clean for the first time that day.

Luke was asleep. Gently, Janna shook him and he opened his eyes and looked at her. Then he sat up slowly, still staring. 'Grief—what a transformation!' he exclaimed. The dress, still damp from the steam, clung to her, emphasising the soft feminine curves she had so sought to hide before. Her arms were slender and long, her legs shapely and tanned, and her hair, still wet, curled round her face, framing it in dark beauty.

He stood up, then he smiled. 'You're a woman all right,' he said. 'No doubt about that. You're beautiful, Janna.'

'Thank you.' His eyes were on her as if he couldn't take them away, and she felt herself going warm. No man had ever looked at her like this before. She felt dizzy and wonderful, all at the same time—and she wanted him to kiss her. Quickly she looked away, ashamed at the madness.

'Your arm,' she said, 'w—won't it be awkward— I mean——'

'Want to help?' he teased. 'No, don't answer. I'll manage.' He opened his case and took out a clean shirt and pants. 'I'll not be long, I'm hungry.' He went into the bathroom and she was alone. She heard the water filling the bath, heard him whistling and went over to close his case. He had left it in disorder, underwear and shirts half out, tumbled about, and she pressed them neatly down and began to close it. A blue piece of paper became dislodged from a pocket in the lid and fluttered to the carpet, and Janna went to pick it up and put it back, and as she did so, she couldn't avoid reading what was written there. It was a simple sheet of expensive notepaper, and it had obviously been in the case for a while, for it was creased and slightly dusty. But the words were very clear.

'Darling Luke,' she read, unable to tear her eyes away, 'hurry home, I miss you so. When you told me over the phone about this latest trip, I nearly died. Why does it always have to be *you* who goes away? Why not Mark? The wedding's not far away now. I trust you'll be home for that! (Ha-ha!) It would hardly be a wedding without you, would it? My thoughts are with you all the time, as you know, and I can't wait for you to hold me again—I'd better stop—some memories are *very*——' the word very was underlined twice—'disturbing, and as I haven't got you *here*. . . .' Janna put the letter back, unable to read further. She felt sick and guilty at having eavesdropped on a letter thus, for it was from a woman who loved him, that was clear. And it was equally obvious that he was getting married when he returned to England. She closed the case and went over to the window. She didn't know why she felt so disturbed by what she had read. She had wanted to tear it up, to burn it, destroy it—and, just for a moment, the strength of her thoughts had frightened her.

She stood very still, calming herself, looking out, and breathing deeply. No wonder he had told her she was safe. He had a lover waiting for him. . . .

'That better?' She hadn't heard the bathroom door open, and turned guiltily to see a clean man looking at her.

'Oh. Yes! Fine,' she said.

'Then let's go down to dinner.' He picked up the

key and put it in his trouser pocket. Janna followed
him to the door, a bright smile on her face to hide
the ache inside her.

They ate in the small dining room, speaking in
Spanish whenever a waiter was within earshot, and
drank wine with their meal and afterwards had
liqueurs with their coffee. The dull ache had eased,
and Janna was feeling quite relaxed when at last
they returned to their room.

Safely inside, Luke locked the door, strode over to
the huge bed, and pulled back the cover. 'One
pillow or two?' he asked her.

'One—but why——'

'Good.' He lifted one pillow off the near side and
placed it firmly in the centre of the bed, half way
down. 'That's the divider. Me one side, you the
other.' He looked at her. 'Okay?'

She nodded. 'I—suppose so.'

'There's no suppose about it. That's how we
sleep. Or would you prefer to be alone in a room?
Did you *see* that greasy waiter staring at you?'

Janna shook her head. 'No.'

'I did. He was undressing you with his eyes.'

'That's a disgusting thing to say!' she gasped,
shocked, and Luke laughed.

'Oh, come on, Janna. You're not *that* naïve, surely.
You didn't honestly see him?'

'No. Honestly!' she said crossly.

'Nor the young buck at the table in the corner?'

'Well, you mean that one with an elderly man?'

'The same. You did?'

'Yes—but he was only looking——'

'Looking—and lusting. If you'd been alone——'
he stopped.

'All right,' she sighed, 'you've made your point.
I'm tired, Luke——'

'So am I. Very tired,' he answered. 'Do you have any nightclothes?'

'A cotton nightie.'

'Go and get undressed in the bathroom. I shan't stare, I promise.' He opened his case and took out a pair of black pyjamas. 'Go on,' he added when she didn't move.

'Luke, are you married?' she asked.

'What?' He smiled. 'No, why?'

'Have you got a girl-friend?'

'Why are you asking? Will it make you feel safer if I say yes?'

'I don't know. I just wondered.' She wanted him to tell her.

'I've a woman friend. Does that answer your question?'

She didn't answer, but turned away and opened her case. Luke came over to her and caught hold of her. 'Does it?' he asked. 'Why did you want to know, Janna?'

'I don't know,' she whispered. She looked at him, wide-eyed, her face pale and tired, and he saw, and said gently:

'You need sleep. We'll talk in the morning.' He gave her a little push. 'Go on, get ready for bed.'

She cleaned her teeth and undressed, and when she went back in, he was already in bed. She switched out the light, and the moon traced a path across the carpet and bed, enabling her to see. She slid between the sheets and the bed was truly huge, and she could feel the dividing pillow, but she was not near him.

'Goodnight, Janna,' he said. He was facing her, his face a grey blur.

'Goodnight.' She lay and waited, and gradually came the sound she wanted to hear as his breathing grew steadier. She was exhausted, but she knew she wouldn't sleep because nothing like this had ever happened to her before. She was sleeping in the same bed as a man she scarcely knew, one she hadn't even known two days ago. And he was all man, virile, tough, strong, like someone out of those dreams of adolescence, vivid and disturbing. Only this was no dream, it was real, and she ached to have him hold her to him, because she knew she was falling in love with him.

She made a small, almost soundless murmur deep in her throat and took hold of the pillow, clutching it to her like some giant cuddly toy that a child might hold. She lay there for a long time, listening to his breathing, looking at the dark shape of him, before she at last fell asleep.

She woke to feel his arms around her and for a moment it seemed a continuation of a delicious, wonderful dream, but it wasn't a dream; his arm was heavy and warm upon her body, and her heart hammered in her breast in sweet anticipation—then she realised that he was still fast asleep, and not aware of his position. The pillow had vanished. She felt it at her feet a moment later—at the same time as she realised that Luke's legs were against her legs, and his body against hers. A heady sense of warmth and love filled her. She didn't want him to wake up. She was so safe, so very safe. . . .

She lay there, with his breath on her face, gentle, faint, and she wondered what he dreamed. It was still dark, but dawn was near, and the room became lighter with every passing minute, so that now she could see him better, see the dark curve of his cheekbone, the blackness of his hair and eyebrows, the shadow of his beard. His mouth curved in a half smile as if his dreams were pleasant ones. She wanted to touch him, to hold him, but she lay still for fear it would disturb him. If time were to stop now, and she had to stay like this for ever, it would not be too much.

'I love you,' she mouthed, silently, and imagined that he heard, and knew, and loved her in return. He didn't, of course. He loved an unknown woman, who wrote on blue paper that she longed for him and remembered. . . . Janna could only imagine what she remembered. She had no memories of anything. . . . But Luke was here, not with the unknown woman but here, with her. And that was all that mattered.

She felt him stir, and closed her eyes quickly. She hoped her heartbeats wouldn't betray her. Goodness, how it hammered! Luke gave a deep throaty murmur, a groan, then she felt his arm move, and she opened her eyes. His were upon her, and he looked stunned.

'Janna——' he said. 'What happened to the pillow?' His voice was husky with sleep and surprise, and she laughed.

'At my feet,' she said. 'I don't know how it got there.' And then she did something that, later, reason told her she should not have done. She slid her arm up, round him, and whispered, 'It's so warm like this, Luke,' and sighed.

'And—dangerous,' he said shakily. 'Look, Janna, I'm sorry——'

She laughed softly. She didn't care. He could have a thousand fiancées. Just for a few minutes surely they wouldn't mind. 'Hold me tight,' she said. 'I'm so safe.'

'No, you're not,' he muttered fiercely. 'Don't you know——'

'I trust you,' she said. 'I was a fool not to. I'm sorry——'

Luke tried to move his arm, to push her away, and she slid her leg over his, and whispered: 'Don't, please—not for a minute——'

'Don't be bloody stupid,' he grated. 'For God's sake, I——' he stopped, and his arm tightened on her waist, then moved, gently, slowly, down to her hip and rested there, then he pulled her to him, and his mouth found hers.

Janna had wondered what it would be like to be kissed by him. At that moment, and in the long, endless minutes that followed, she knew. She knew, at last, the sweet taste of his mouth, his lips exploring her mouth, his hand caressing her slim soft body, and she moaned, a small sound of happiness of longing for she knew not what, except that nothing he could do would be wrong.

She raised her head to his face, then his neck, and responded to the kisses with an abandon she didn't really understand, not even then——

'Janna, love,' he whispered, and his voice shook, and he was trembling. 'For God's sake, you don't know what you're doing to me—let me go before it's too late——'

'Too late for what?' she murmured, and took his hand to guide it to her breast. 'Feel my heart, feel how it beats—Oh, Luke, Luke,' she whispered. 'I didn't know——'

He jerked his hand away as if her skin burned him, then, as if unable to help himself, put it back to cup the soft roundness in his palm. He gave a long shuddering groan, and began to ease her nightdress off, and she helped him, and flung it on the covers, then lay on her back, revelling in his touch which was hard and teasing, gentle and tender—and which brought her to the very brink of desire until she cried out to him and held him close to her so that their bodies burned with intense heat, and she knew he was going to make love to her. . . .

There was a dreadful cry, as of pain, and Luke wrenched himself free and staggered out of the bed, and fell. Janna sat up, feeling as if one half of her had been torn away, and saw him crouched down as if in agony. 'Luke——' She slid out of bed and ran to him and knelt beside him. The air was cool to her bare skin. He pushed away, violently. 'Don't touch me,' he muttered. 'Leave me——'

She stood up as if he had struck her violently, and he staggered to his feet and looked at her, shaking as if with a fever. 'Don't touch me,' he said again. 'I *beg* of you, Janna, don't come *near* me.'

He was breathing as if he had been running for miles, and she backed away, fearful, and grabbed her nightdress and put it on. She too was trembling now. Luke went to the window and drank in the air, as if to cool himself, and he was gradually regaining control, for when she went to him he didn't push her away. He looked at her instead.

'I was going to make love to you,' he said. 'Don't you understand? Are you so naïve? I was going to *make love* to you—and in another moment it would have been too late.' She stared at him, wide-eyed, wordless, and he grated: 'Don't look at me like that!'

'I—wanted——' her face crumpled, and she felt the hot streaming tears fill her eyes and brim over. 'I only wanted——' but she didn't know what it was she had only wanted.

His breathing was still harsh, but he was clearly past the point of explosion. 'It doesn't work that way,' he said huskily. 'Mother Nature has a trick of coming up behind you and knocking you on the head sometimes. You nearly——' He stopped. 'I'm going to have a cold bath—I need one.' He walked like a man in a dream, like a man in pain, towards the bathroom door, and Janna watched him go. She hugged her arms to her sides, then she went over to the bed and sat down. Reason was returning, and she could begin to think again, and she realised then, belatedly, what had so nearly happened—She went hot with the shame that filled her. What had possessed her to behave as she had? Some madness had overcome her, and she didn't fully understand, even now, the implications. The water ran, but now Luke wasn't whistling. He came out minutes later, hair dripping wet, only his pyjama trousers on, and looked at her. His face was very serious. He held a towel in his hand and began to rub his hair vigorously.

Janna watched him, and he walked over to the bed, and she instinctively flinched, as if he might strike her. He sat down beside her. 'Janna,' he said, 'it was a mistake. You were right, we should never have slept in the same bed. I'm sorry.'

'Sorry?' she whispered. She hugged herself and rocked back and forth in her anguish and misery. 'You hate me, don't you?'

'How can I do that?' he said, wonderingly.

'I know you do.' She began to sob helplessly, putting her face in her hands, and he groaned.

'Don't cry, for God's sake! Please don't cry, Janna.' He put his arm round her. 'Sweet child, don't you know why I couldn't—why I mustn't?' He held her close, but in an almost impersonal way. 'You're so young, and innocent—I couldn't do that to you, knowing—listen, love, I'm fifteen years older than you. Fifteen. Nearly twice your age. I would have regretted it so much, after—don't you see?' He gave a deep sigh. 'I can't take the chance again. We'll share a room, but not a bed, in future. You need looking after, not turning into a woman before you're ready. You're not ready yet, and when that day comes it will be with the right man for you— someone you've chosen, whom you love, and who loves you.' He smiled as he tilted her chin up. 'You'll never know how noble I feel at this moment—and how damned virtuous—and how I wish I didn't!' He laughed softly. 'You'll never know. And perhaps just as well.'

Janna trembled within his arms. This—this was so different from what had gone before. A world away from the ecstasy of him holding her, and yet in a way, even more beautiful. Luke was tender, and gentle, and his face held such concern that she had to smile, to reassure him.

'You're right,' she whispered. 'I'm sorry I was so—so——' He put his finger to her lips.

'Hush! Don't apologise for anything. You were *you*—you were warm, and passionate, and all woman, believe me.' He sighed. 'Yes, all woman. Some man is going to be very lucky, some day.' He squeezed her arm. 'Come on, we'd better get dressed. I think my hand is steady enough to get shaved now.' He held it out. 'Just about.'

As she stood up, he caught her arm. 'Wait, Janna—we're going to have to talk, before we leave here.'

She stood there, quite still, and looked at him. His face was very serious. 'Now?' she asked.

'No.' He grinned faintly. 'Not now, when you're dressed, and I'm dressed. It's easier that way.'

She felt a sense of dread. 'What about?' she whispered.

'I'll tell you when you're washed and dressed.
I've got to get it clear in my mind. But it's to do
with going back to England.'

'Please——' she began, and he cut in.

'No. Later. When you're dressed.'

Janna ran into the bathroom. Her heart was
pounding. What on earth was he going to say?

CHAPTER FIVE

When both were fully dressed, and Luke had
shaved, and combed his wet hair, he said to Janna:
'Sit down on the bed.'

'Yes, Luke.' She sat down, and he pulled up a
chair in front of her.

'How would you like to go back to England with
me, by plane?' he asked.

She looked at him, unable to grasp what he was
saying. 'What?' she said. He repeated it, slowly. 'Is
this a joke?' she whispered.

'No, I'm deadly serious. I can't go on—with you.
I can't leave you either—and I don't think you'd
get a passport as easily as you think. But I have a
plan.' He rubbed his forehead. 'I want you to listen,
and not interrupt until I've finished. Promise?'

She nodded. 'I promise.'

'Right. I've been here before, several times. I
know how it is in these places—anywhere in South
America, for that matter,—to get things done. It's
murder. But you have your birth certificate, and I
know a man in local government here. He's been a
useful contact in the past—we've got a factory not

twenty miles away, and I've got an account here
in a bank—and I think I could get you fixed up,
but——' he hesitated, 'there's only one way to get it
done in under a couple of months—and it would
mean us getting married.' Janna opened her mouth,
promise forgotten, and he said: 'Wait, *listen*. It
would be a marriage of convenience, simply to get
you out of here fast. We can have it annulled immediately we reach England, then I'd fly back here
and take up where I left off. That way you're safe,
where you want to be, and I'm alone, as I planned
to be. Janna, let's be realistic. I can't travel much
further with you—not now, not after—this,' he indi-
cated the bed. 'I thought it over while I had that cold
bath. It sharpens the wits wonderfully, does cold
water! I'll see my friend today, talk it over, sort it
out, and we'll take it from there. Now, you can speak.'

'But I can't marry you,' she whispered. 'You——'
How could she tell him she had read the letter? She
couldn't. 'You can't make this sacrifice—and in any
case, I thought you were nearly at that man's——'

'That can wait, at least a few weeks. Is the idea of
being married to me, even in name only, so repel-
lent?'

She managed to smile. If only he *knew*! 'No, of
course not. But I can't let you—what will everyone
think?'

'They won't know. We don't have to tell anyone,'
he said. 'Why should we?'

That was logical. No one need know. She had no
one to know anyway, and she didn't know his circumstances. 'Thank you,' she whispered. 'I can't
thank you enough——' Her voice broke.

'Don't,' he said, and knelt before her. 'When we
get to England I'll take you to my mother's home,

near London. You can stay there while you try and
trace your relatives—and we've a very discreet solicitor friend who'll arrange for the annulment.'

Janna nodded. 'Why are you doing this for me?'
she asked quietly.

He grinned. 'Because you felt sorry for me and
gave me extra food that night, remember?'

She laughed, and Luke stood up and pulled her
to her feet. 'Come on, let's have breakfast. I'll leave
you at the shops buying a few dresses, and go and
see old Luis.' He kissed her lightly, on her forehead,
a butterfly kiss, a world removed from the others,
and they went down to the dining room.

That night Luke slept on the floor, rolled in the
sheets, and lying on a blanket. Janna lay and listened to his breathing before she too fell asleep. It
had been a very busy day. They were to be married
on the following Sunday, three days away, and two
days after that she would have a passport.

Within a week from now she would be in England. It seemed totally unbelievable, and she
pinched herself surreptitiously under the bedclothes.
It hurt. It was real.

Luke had told her more about his home, where
she would be going to stay for a while, until she
discovered her relatives—if any. She would never
be able to pay him back, she knew that, but she
would try. During the time she would be staying at
Courthill, his home, a discreet annulment of their
marriage would make her a free woman. The one
who had written him the letter would never even
know. . . .

She wondered how he would explain Janna to
her. Surely, if he were planning to get married soon,
he would have told Janna? He could hardly do so

before the annulment anyway. How would he explain *that* to his other fiancée? She wished, drowsily, as sleep claimed her, that she hadn't seen the letter in the case.

The following morning they went out shopping. Luke bought her a simple gold ring which she would wear until they reached England. She would then remove it and put it with the wooden cross from Brother Marcos. And when the time came for them to part, as it would, she would have one small souvenir of him. It was Friday, and her wedding was the day after next, at a small church near the hotel. It would be a Catholic ceremony, because there were no Protestant churches in Rio d'Oro, and the only guests, and witnesses, would be Luis and his wife. There would be no ceremony after, just a simple dinner at a hotel belonging to a friend of Luis. Janna suspected that it had cost Luke a lot to have the wedding, and therefore the passport, arranged so expeditiously, but when she had asked him about it, his answer had been vague and dismissive. She knew he was wealthy—how wealthy, she wasn't to find out until they reached England.

The clothes in the shops in the Avenida were expensive, she could see that by window-shopping, and she exclaimed, 'Good grief! I can't buy any of these!'

'You have to have a wedding dress, you idiot,' Luke told her. 'And sandals, and a bag. And buy something simple that will do for in England.'

'You'll have to guide me,' she answered. 'I don't know what *will* do in England.' He was pleasant and relaxed, as if, now he had made the decision to take her back, some big problem had been solved. Janna knew she would be grateful to him for the rest of her life. She would also love him for the rest of her life, but that was one thing he would never know. She wasn't part of his life. He was a wonderful man, a kind, gentle, strong man, and she hoped that the woman he loved, and who professed to love him, appreciated that fact. She might even meet her. . . .

And then it was Sunday, and her wedding day. She woke feeling absurdly happy that morning, which was ridiculous, because it was a mere formality to enable her to achieve her dream of getting to England, but she would legally—even if only for a matter of weeks—be married to the man she loved. There would be one other difference between theirs and a normal marriage, but only she and Luke knew that. It would not be consummated. And when she met his mother, it would not be as his bride, but as a girl who had needed help. His mother wouldn't even know that Janna was her daughter-in-law.

The ceremony was beautiful though simple, and Janna found out for the first time, as they signed the register, what her new name was. Luke had told her that Tallon wasn't his real name—he had simply forgotten to tell her his real one. She was Mrs Lucas Hayes-Ross. She tasted the name, said it softly to herself, as he kissed her lightly on the cheek and asked:

'How does it feel?'

'Being Mrs Hayes-Ross?' She smiled. 'Very pleasant.'

'Good. Let's go and see our guests.' Luis Domingo and his wife were tall, good-looking, dark-skinned Argentinians, both charming. They had six children, Luke had told her, two of whom were at university, three married, and one son still at home.

Elegant and very pleasant, they made the dinner that followed a meal of laughter and enjoyment, and Eva Domingo took Janna to one side as the men went to the rear of the restaurant and said:

'You make a beautiful bride, Janna. I am so happy to meet you—You and Luke are travelling to England on Wednesday, I believe?'

'Yes,' Janna smiled.

'And are you going on honeymoon, my dear?'

'No—not until later. We're staying at a small hotel, the Negresco, till then.'

Eva wrinkled her nose. 'That's no place for your wedding night!' she protested. It seemed, Janna thought in dismay, as if she and her husband didn't know the true facts of the arrangement. 'No place at all! You must come and stay with us, my dear, until your flight. I insist.' Then, as the men returned to their table, laughing over something, she raised her voice slightly. 'Luis, we cannot let these two children stay at the Negresco! They must stay with us.' She smiled at Janna. 'Our house is very large—we have a guest bedroom that is quite, *quite* private.'

'It's very kind of you, Eva,' Luke answered. 'But I wouldn't put you to the trouble——'

'It's no trouble!' Her look, at her husband, said that the matter was settled. 'You men can go now and collect your luggage while we wait here and have some more champagne, then we will go and have a little party at home.'

Luis grinned and turned to Luke. 'I do not argue with my wife,' he said, 'not if I wish for a peaceful life. Come, my friend.' He took Luke's arm, and they went out.

That seemed to be that. Only it wasn't. Eva looked at Janna and gave a mysterious smile. 'I think,' she said, 'that I have a few phone calls to make——' Her eyes shone with genuine delight, and she beckoned a waiter, who came rushing over.

'I want a telephone, please,' she said.

Janna put her hand on the other's arm. 'Please—you mustn't go to all this trouble,' she protested, but Eva laughed, a glorious, full-throated laugh.

'It's no trouble!' she said. 'I love parties. And what better excuse?'

A telephone was brought, plugged in, and Eva began phoning. Janna had lost count by the time the two men returned, and looked helplessly at Luke, who shrugged.

He sat down. 'We're having a party?' he asked.

'It seems so.'

'There!' Eva beckoned for the waiter to take the telephone away, and beamed at them. 'All is arranged. I think we had better leave now——'

Luis shrugged, looked at Luke as if to say—what can I do? and they went out to his car. Luke's Land Rover was parked beside it. As they drove out, following Luis's Mercedes, he said to Janna: 'I'm leaving this at their house until I get back.'

Until I get back, he said. And that was what he would do. Escort her to England, go all that incredible distance with her, and then return. She didn't want him to do that. She was frightened for him. She was also his wife. It was strange to think that she was now married. She fingered the gold band that she wore, and it was solid and warm and reassuring. Vague ideas began to form in her head, tenuous and insubstantial, barely more than a drifting of thought——

'Why go to England yet?'

'What?' He was concentrating on following Luis

through the heavy evening traffic, not really listening.

'I said, why go to England on Wednesday?
Why not let me stay with you, and go with you to
this——'

'No.' He said it firmly, quickly. 'It's quite impossible.'

'But I'm frightened.'

'Frightened? Of staying in England at my home?'

'Not that—for *you*.'

'I'm touched by your concern, but you don't need
to be, Janna. I haven't come all this way to be
thwarted at the last minute.' He looked briefly at
her. 'Don't you see, I've spent all these weeks track-
ing him down, and he's not two days' journey from
here.'

'From here? Is that all?'

'Yes.'

'Then you knew, roughly, how far it would be
when you picked me up?'

'Yes.'

'And if you hadn't found out I was a woman,
we'd be there now?'

'Got it in one.'

'Instead of which——'

'I married you. Quite a difference, eh?'

'It's not a laughing matter,' she said, quavery-
voiced.

'I never said it was. I was pointing out that I've
delayed *my* intentions somewhat, simply to get *you*
to England——'

'But *how* are you going to steal it from him?' she
burst out.

'I've a letter of introduction—in the name of
Luke Tallon—from a very well known philatelist in

London. It's forged, naturally, but by the time he finds out, it'll be too late. I've brought some stamps with me——'

'Where?'

'Where do you think? How much room do you think stamps take, for God's sake? I've got a couple of dozen tucked away in my wallet. He won't be able to resist them.'

'But—how——' Bewildered, Janna shook her head.

'I've also brought a perfect copy of this—*my*—Cape Triangular. *That* he won't see until it's in his possession.' Luke smiled softly and Janna shivered.

'You—you told me you hadn't thought of anything,' she whispered.

'I didn't know you. I've never had any doubt in my mind about what I was going to do.'

'Take me with you. I—it will look more genuine, if you're married—and we are. I can—distract him at the crucial moment—I can do it.'

'You didn't approve before. You thought, if I remember rightly, that to make a fuss about a piece of paper was ridiculous——'

'I've changed my mind,' she cut in. 'I want to help you.'

'I believe you do.' He sounded surprised.

'Please, Luke!' She put her hand on his arm.

'We'll talk about it tomorrow, after this damned party. I promise—We'll talk about it.'

Janna realised she would have to be content with that, and relaxed, or tried to. They were driving along a wide road, with large mansions spread out at either side, hidden behind tall hedges. Here all was peace and calm, the ordered calm of the very wealthy. The Mercedes slowed down, its rear indicator lights winking steadily, and Luke did the same. They swept up a broad tree-lined drive, and a man stepped out from the shadows by the gate and closed them behind the Land Rover. They stopped outside a large white house, brilliantly lit, with wrought iron doors outside the front entrance, and tall windows with open green shutters and window baskets full of exotic flowers.

Eva came over as Janna climbed out, eyes wide. She had never even *seen* a house like this before, let alone been in one.

'Welcome to our home,' smiled Eva. 'We'll let the men put the cars away while we go in. Come along, my dear.'

'Your house is beautiful,' Janna murmured.

'Thank you! Let me show you your room. I think you will be not unpleased.'

The doors swung back silently, and a woman stood there dressed in severe black, nodding to her employer, and bowing slightly as Eva introduced the housekeeper. Eva told the woman that Señora Hayes-Ross was their guest, that she and her husband would be staying in the Pink Suite, and that flowers were to be taken there as soon as possible.

The housekeeper listened impassively, assured Eva that the matter would be attended to immediately, and left them.

'Come into the *salón*, Janna.' Eva drifted across the magnificent hall, with its black floor and stands full of flowers and ferns, and white silk hangings. They entered a large room, all whites and golds, the colours echoed in carpets, furniture, curtains and walls. The effect was one of magnificence and sheer luxury.

Janna sank down into the white leather settee, marvelling at it all. She had lived all her nineteen years in a simple four-roomed bungalow whose furnishings were plain and serviceable. She had been happy, because she had known no different. She was discovering now that there was another life style, one she hadn't even envisaged. A smartly dressed manservant came in, and Eva asked him to serve champagne. As he was about to go out she added: 'Oh, and by the way, Pedro, we are having a party later. Please see to the food.'

That was that. A party arranged, impromptu, no rushing around for Eva. Janna sat there, wide-eyed, listening, bemused.

When, some short while later, she was with Luke in the bedroom they were to occupy, she told him, and he smiled. 'That's the way they do it here,' he said. 'You can bet there are a dozen people scurrying round now getting food prepared, putting bottles of wine to cool—or warm, according.' He looked round. 'Nice room.'

It was an understatement. The room was opulent, with a large fourposter bed, and heavy antique furniture that reflected years of loving care and polish. The walls were faint pink, and there was a large bowl of exotic flowers on a table by the window. Far away, and below, the lights of Rio d'Oro twinkled, and the sky was black velvet studded with hundreds of glittering diamonds. Janna rubbed her bare toes in a white fur rug by the bed, and stretched.

'Better get ready,' said Luke. 'Wear that white dress I bought you.'

She looked at him. 'I thought you wanted me to save that for England?'

'I did—but I didn't know there'd be a party tonight.' He looked at her solemnly. 'I'm sorry, I couldn't get out of it. But we don't need to stay late—they'll expect us to want to sneak off.' He gave a dry smile, and she felt a warm tide of colour suffuse her face.

She turned away. 'I suppose so.' She bit her lip. 'I'll get showered and changed.' Their bathroom led directly off from the bedroom. It was large, pink-tiled from floor to ceiling, and a startling contrast to the one at the Negresco—pink tub, shower, and all the fittings were gold. She went in, looked, and exclaimed: 'Wow! Look at this!'

Luke followed her in, and stood behind her, laughing. 'Hmm, posh is the word, wouldn't you say?'

'I'll say!' She looked round at him, eyes shining. 'I've never even *seen* anything like this before,' she said in awe.

He looked at her with an odd expression on his face, and she felt suddenly warm. Then he moved away and went out. She watched him go, her heart bumping rapidly. For an absurd moment she had wanted him to kiss her—and, equally, it had seemed that he might. She closed the door slowly.

For an impromptu party, it was a wild success. If it had been planned for weeks, it could hardly have run more smoothly. The atmosphere, from the first guests arriving at ten until Janna crept away, exhausted, at three in the morning, was one of warmth and friendliness. She was accorded great respect as the new bride, and Luke was treated like visiting royalty. She realised at one point during the evening, when for a few minutes she was alone in a comparatively quiet corner, that he fitted in superbly well to this kind of scene. It was his world, they were his kind of people. There was simply no comparison with the tall dark attractive man who was amusing three young matrons—they hanging on to his every word—and the rough tramp who had come into Señora Lopez' bar for a meal. Janna watched him— her husband—unobserved. She wondered, not for the first time, why he had chosen to help her. There was no obligation on him at all. What was it Brother Marcos had said? She tried to recall the exact words. 'Luke, I feel, is a good man——' He had said that, and he was a clear-sighted man, a shrewd one. Of course, Luke was a good man, but he was not of her world. And she could never in a million years be part of his. For a brief time, perhaps, in England, and then it would be goodbye. She touched her wedding ring, and a smiling man came over and raised his glass to her.

'Señora!' he said reproachfully. 'You are the belle of the ball, and you stand here alone! How can your husband allow that?'

She laughed, the mood of introspection vanishing in the face of his dazzling smile, and answered something amusing, and the moment of sadness passed.

The music blared out, and couples danced; Janna and Luke did a sedate waltz at nearly three, and she told him she was tired.

'So am I,' he said. 'You go—I'll follow after I've excused us to Eva and Luis. They won't mind.' He kissed her forehead lightly. 'I'll be up in ten minutes.'

He meant so that she could get ready for bed in privacy. He was going to sleep on the easy chair in their room. That had been the first arrangement they had made.

She slipped away, and the noise followed, but getting fainter as she made her way along the wide corridor that led to their bedroom. It was, as Eva had said, practically separate from the rest of the house, and when she went in and closed the door behind her she could hear nothing save the faintest boom-boom of the record being played. Certainly nothing to keep her awake. The drive was lined with expensive cars, but that was at the front of the house. The room overlooked the pool and gardens at the rear, and all was silent and still.

It was a very warm night. Janna showered and dressed in the pale blue satin nightdress she had bought, and got into bed. Ten minutes had passed, and a few moments later came a tap at the door. 'Janna? Are you in bed?'

'Yes.'

Luke came in, loosening his tie and taking off his jacket. He kicked off his shoes. 'God, I'm shattered,' he muttered, and sat on the edge of the bed and rubbed his arm. 'This damn thing itches.'

She had forgotten about the bandage. 'Shall I do it now?' she asked.

'Would you? The stitches are irritating. It was so damned hot down there, even with the air-conditioning going full blast.'

'Of course.' Janna slipped out of bed and put on the matching negligee. The silk was cool to her skin. 'Take off your shirt.' He did so, and she took the first aid box from the drawer and went to sit beside him, on his left side. 'Why don't you have a shower first?' she suggested. 'You'll feel cooler.'

He looked at her. 'Are you sober?' he asked.

'Yes.' She stared back at him in surprise. 'I stuck to fruit juice all evening. I'd had enough champagne at dinner. I'm not used to drink, remember?'

He grinned faintly. 'Clever girl! I'll have a king-sized hangover in the morning—no, it's morning now—when I wake up, I mean.'

'Serves you right,' she said primly, and he winced.

'Ouch! Are you nagging me?'

'No.' She laughed. 'Of course not. You've got aspirin in your first aid box. Want a couple?'

'I wouldn't mind.' He rubbed his temples and gave a huge yawn. She went to fetch the aspirin, and filled a glass with the mineral water that had been left for them, tap water not being safe to drink, unless boiled. She looked at Luke as he drank it, and felt a pang of sympathy. He had been plied with champagne all evening, and had undoubtedly drunk more than his fair share, as the groom, and therefore one half of the guests of honour.

'Look,' she said, 'you can't sleep on that chair. You have the bed—I'll sleep on it instead.'

He looked at her, a faint grin on his face. 'I believe you mean it.'

'Of course I do. It won't be so bad for me. I'm smaller, and thinner. I can practically curl up like a mouse on it. You'll be sprawling all over——'

'You paint a pretty picture,' he commented. 'Sprawl? Are you implying I'm huge?'

'You're far from dainty,' she retorted. 'I bet you weigh twice as much as me.'

He laughed. 'There's a thought. What do you weigh?'

She knew, because there had been a weighing machine in the restaurant that evening. She told him the weight in kilograms and Luke did a hasty calculation and said: 'Good grief! Eight and a half stone!'

'And?'

He shook his head. 'Not double, but not so

damned far off. I weigh fifteen stone. But let me remind you, madame, I'm a damned sight taller.'

'I can see that. How tall?'

'Six feet three, nearly two metres. And you're only a little shrimp of——' He weighed her up and down. 'No, you're not. You're really quite tall, for a girl, aren't you?'

'Yes. Aren't the women tall in England?'

'The average is about five-five—you're, let me see, five-eight or nine—that's taller than average. My mother's about your height, though.' He sighed. 'You'll like her.'

'Tell me about her,' she said.

'Not now, love,' he yawned again. 'I'm too tired.'

'Go and get your shower. I'll do your arm, you'll sleep in the bed. And please hurry, I'm nearly falling asleep myself.'

Luke groaned and got up, and when, after only minutes, he came back, dressed only in pyjama trousers, she put a clean dressing and bandage on his arm, after inspecting it carefully. It was healing nicely, the skin a healthy colour, but slightly tight around the stitches. After applying the soothing ointment he told her that it was much easier.

'In you get,' she ordered, and pulled back the covers.

'I don't like——' he began.

'Get *in*!'

He pulled a face and scrambled in. 'Look,' he said, 'I've an idea—er—I don't know how to put it, but—couldn't you—or I—sleep on top of one sheet, the other one beneath it?'

'I don't know what you mean,' she said, shaking her head.

'Oh, hell,' he groaned, and got out again. 'Like

this.' He pulled back the sheet, the thin cover on top, and pointed. 'Get in.'

She did so, and he put the sheet over her, then got in the other side so that he was on top of the sheet but under the cover. 'See?'

She laughed. 'I see.'

He got in and pulled the cover up. 'No danger,' he said, 'and now I'm going to sleep. Goodnight, Janna.' So saying, he turned his back to her, pulled the cover up, and fell immediately fast asleep. Janna pulled the light cord and the room was plunged into darkness. She was with him, but not with him. It was safe, and sensible, and such a simple idea. She wondered why they had not thought of it before. On that thought she fell asleep.

She woke up because she couldn't breathe properly, and found out why. Luke was sprawled well across her, dead to the world, and she was all tangled up in the sheet. She eased herself slightly away, which enabled her to pull the sheet freer, and he didn't stir. Feeling warm, safe and comfortable, she lay there, half beneath him, with only the sheet as a barrier, and went back to sleep, to rejoin a most interesting and colourful dream. . . .

CHAPTER SIX

It was Luke who woke up first, and by his movements woke Janna. He lay leaning on his elbow just beside her head, and said, 'Hi!'

'Hi. How's your hangover?' She lay back on the pillow and smiled sleepily at him, surfacing from some lovely place where she had been with him.

He groaned. 'Don't say that word!'

'All right, I won't. How's your head?' His face was only inches away. He seemed to be studying her nose, although she couldn't be sure.

'Terrible. Do you know you've got freckles?'

'Yes, thanks, I did know.' His left arm lay across her, but he didn't seem to be aware of it. It was at a most respectable angle across her waist, under the top cover, but over the sheet which covered her and didn't cover him. 'We must sleep this way more often,' she said.

'Quite so.' He nodded, and then winced. 'Ouch, I shouldn't have done that!'

'Why? Did it hurt?'

'Yes.'

'Shall I get you some more aspirin?'

'No, not yet, I don't want to move just yet. I'm very comfortable.'

'You don't look it, propped up on your pillow like that.'

'Don't I?' He seemed surprised. Then, moving his right arm under her neck, and lying down so that his head touched hers, he asked: 'Is that better?'

'Mmm.' She wished he wouldn't. His left arm, the bandaged one, still lay across her stomach, but with his right hand he was touching her ear.

'Pretty ears,' he said. 'Quite pretty.'

'I'm glad you approve.'

He leaned forward, just that inch needed, and kissed her soft mouth, and murmured, after a moment or two: 'Pretty mouth as well, very— nice.'

Janna couldn't breathe, but this time it wasn't because she was tangled in a sheet, it was for an entirely different reason.

'Look,' she said weakly, 'I don't think you ought to be——'

'There is no possible way I can make love to you, lying like this,' he said, whispering the words in her ear. 'No way. A sheet makes a very effective barrier—and anyway, I couldn't.'

'Why not?' she asked, and added hastily: 'Not that I want to know—I mean——'

'Because my head is giving me *hell*,' he groaned. 'That's why.'

'Poor thing!' She put up her hand and touched the back of his head, then pulled it down to rest on her shoulder. With her other hand she began to gently massage the back of his neck.

He groaned, but it was more an appreciative one than of pain. 'Mmm,' he said, after some moments. 'Nice—don't stop.'

'I won't,' she soothed. Her hands were gentle and skilful. She reached down slightly with her other hand and rubbed gently across his shoulders. She could feel the hard muscles under the skin—and the tension.

'Please,' she said, 'just relax. Your headache will go, you'll see.' Luke shrugged himself into a more comfortable position and gave himself up to her ministrations. She had never been so happy. She knew she was helping him, that he was enjoying her massage, and she could feel the muscles of his back slowly becoming less tense.

After some minutes he muttered sleepily: 'This is marvellous. You should be a masseuse, your hands are so—mmm——' his voice tailed off.

Janna shook with silent laughter. Gradually, by easing her body upwards slightly, she was able to extend her touch along his back, and he made a little murmur of sheer contentment, almost a deep purr, like some jungle cat. Almost absentmindedly, and she was quite sure he wasn't aware of it, his left hand moved upwards until it was resting on her breast. She faltered for a moment, her pulses throbbing, then, taking a discreet deep breath, began rubbing again. Luke's fingers curved round her breast, cupping it, then were still. Janna went on, because to stop now would be to betray her confusion.

'Is that better?' she managed to say, after a few minutes longer.

'Fantastic. But your poor arms must be aching. Have a rest.'

'Thanks,' she said drily, and he laughed very softly, turned, and bit her ear. Then, almost as if it were inevitable, his lips trailed across her cheek to her mouth. Time was lost as they kissed for endless, beautiful minutes, and he stroked her breast very gently, and whispered: 'Dear Janna, I want so much to make love to you——'

'That's very obvious,' she said shakily. She trembled in his arms and tasted the sweetness of his mouth, and her body ached with a fierce longing for him, a continuation of her dream.

'But I won't—dear God, I mustn't, and I won't. You're so safe——'

She held him tightly, and heard his groan of pain, then his mouth found hers again, and they were clinging to each other, on fire with the heat of desire, and the mutual longing. Then Luke muttered, after minutes in which it was obvious that his control was nearly lost, 'Please, let me go—I can't——'

'No!' she cried fiercely, and raked her fingernails across his back.

'Oh, God——' he cried out, and there were salty

tears on her lips, and she didn't know whether they were her own or his, and it didn't matter. 'Help me!' He fell away from her, fighting desperately to control himself, his breathing harsh and ragged, and put his hand out to her face. 'No,' he whispered, 'I promised—Janna——'

She licked the palm of his hand, moist with sweat, and he took it away as if he had touched fire, and been burned. She caught hold of him, then they were a tangle of arms and legs, and she knew he had no strength to fight her, and she felt dizzy and light-headed, revelling in her power. He lay back panting, face and body drenched in perspiration, eyes nearly black, his pupils dilated, and he looked at her as she leaned over him—then, with what must have been a superhuman effort, he wrenched himself free and stumbled to his feet, pulling her after him.

'No, Janna,' he said, and to speak was a great effort. 'For God's sake, no—I can't fight——' He was shaking, and he held her in his arms, as though to steady himself. She began to cry, a cry of despair and sadness, and he moved away, staggered to the window and leaned against the glass, his body heaving with emotion. 'Don't,' he said. 'Don't——'

She followed him, eyes filled with blinding tears, hating him—*hating* him. Scarcely aware of what she was doing, she lashed out at his bare back and pummelled him until he turned round and caught her flailing fists, and there was agony on his face. 'Stop!' he ordered sharply.

For answer she wrenched herself free and caught him a stinging blow across his mouth, then another, and another, and he stood there like a man who can take no more, but couldn't stop her, rocking slightly as each blow struck him.

'I hate you!' she breathed. 'Hate you! You're not

a man, d'you hear me—not a man———!' She began to laugh, and she couldn't stop, and she loathed him, and it was all there in her face for him to see. The hurt, the longing, the aching for him. She reached up, to wipe the look of agony from his face, and he caught her wrist, and she struggled. 'Don't you *hear* me?' she gasped, the laughter now a choking sobbing. 'You're not a *man*———'

She saw his face change, and she had gone too far, but it was too late to stop now. Her legs buckled beneath her and he pulled her to her feet. He had reached the end of his tether. He gave an animal cry and with one hand caught her nightdress and ripped it straight down the front, then picked her up, walked over to the bed and threw her on it.

He was beyond all control—too late, she saw that, too late—and much, much too late to stop him.

They lay together on the bed, and it was much later, and Janna had no more tears to shed. Bruised, aching, she lay beside him, unable to move away, and Luke put out his hand and touched her face. 'Forgive me,' he said, his voice broken and husky.

She turned towards him, saw the agony in his eyes, and whispered: 'I drove you to it, Luke—forgive *me*.'

'Oh, Janna!' He stroked her face very gently. 'Don't look at me like that. Dear God, you don't know how I feel!'

'It's all right.' She was the strong one at this moment, the comforter. She drew his head towards her. 'It's all right,' she whispered.

He lay, head on her breast, a man who had reached the limits of endurance and beyond. He was suffering, she knew that. Gently she stroked his head. Tears filled her eyes, and he lifted his head, as he heard her choking breath, and his mouth trembled. 'Don't——' he began.

'I—can't—help it.' She was shaking now, help-less, trembling as much as he. Luke took her and held her cradled in his arms like a child, and grad-ually, as the minutes passed, he began stroking her, soothing her, gentling her so that the tears died away and were gone, and it was he was the stronger, he the comforter. Janna gave herself up to his strength, to the warm and gentleness of his hands, and he kissed her, and the kiss was salty tasting, and yet sweet, and far, far more tender than anything she had ever known before. So gradually that neither were aware of the point at which it became different, the atmosphere changed, and a warmth filled them. She reached up to touch his face, and it was gentle now, so gentle, and their eyes met and held for a long instant of time, and awareness. Luke slid his hand to her breast, then leaned down to kiss it.

Without haste, without any urgency, because there was no urgency, not any more, he slid his arms round her unresisting body, and the warmth grew to a fire, and their murmured words, softly uttered, were a spoken confirmation of what both needed to know. Gently this time, he led her along the way they were going to go, and in this was such gent-leness that all other memories became so blurred and amorphous as mist, and were eased away, to vanish as mist did, without trace—touch, feeling, warm emotions that filled her, as Luke led her to-wards the final fulfilment with great skill and care, until at last she cried out, not in pain, but in ecstasy, and knew at last, the hidden secrets of love.

Luke looked at her as they dressed. The day was not

young, it was nearly noon, but no one had come to disturb them. Janna found her sandals and put them on, sitting on the bed, and saw Luke watching her. He was pulling on his shirt, and when it was on, and as he buttoned up, he said:

'There's nothing I can say that will alter things now, Janna, but I want you to know that I didn't intend it to happen.'

'I know. I'm as much to blame as you——' she faltered. 'It won't alter anything—it's all right, you know.'

He closed his eyes. 'It's not that easy,' he said wearily. 'We can hardly have our marriage annulled.'

'No one else will know,' she said fiercely. '*I promise.*' She looked at him. 'Don't you *see*? Once we're in England I'll just be Janna Thorne again. This— interlude—will be over.' She blinked. 'I know my world isn't yours. I'll find my own relatives—you have your life to lead, and I'll have mine.' She gave a smile. 'One day I'll find a way of repaying all your help. I doubt if I'd have reached England for a long time if it hadn't been for you. I'll never forget that.'

'You owe me nothing,' he said harshly. He ran his fingers through his hair. 'You seem to be missing what I'm trying to say. Janna, it shouldn't have been *me*.'

'Well, it was,' she answered. 'I'm not sorry. I won't pretend I am—does that make me sound terrible?' She stood up. 'If it does, I'm sorry for that. But your—girl-friend will never know. You have my word on that.'

'Girl-friend?' he queried.

It was time to confess. 'I saw—accidentally—a letter from your case. It fell out—I'm sorry, but I read part of it.'

'Oh, God!'

'I shouldn't have, I know. I'm sorry. You—you're planning to get married——'

'We were.' He gave a wry smile. 'But for obvious reasons it will have to be postponed.'

'I know. Don't you see why I feel guilty? You did this, for me—how can I ever repay that debt?' She gave him a bright smile. 'Is she beautiful?'

'Yes.'

'What does she look like? Will I meet her?'

'To your second question—yes, you probably will. She lives near my home. To your first, she's very blonde—as fair as you're dark, and she's tall—as tall as you, slim, very attractive. Her name's Annabel.' He sighed. 'I've known her nearly all my life. She's twenty-nine.'

'Won't she wonder what I'm doing with you?'

'I'll tell her something. She's not the jealous type.' No, but I am, thought Janna with sudden dismay. I've not even met her, and I don't like her.

'Is she—have you——' She bit her lip.

'Yes, we have,' he said evenly.

'Oh.' She turned away. 'I'm sorry, I shouldn't have asked that.'

'No, you shouldn't, but you did.' Luke put on his shoes. 'We'd better go.'

And I suppose she's better than *me*, she wanted to shout. She hurt inside, a deep wounding pain in her heart. For a time, for an hour, Luke had been hers, and the love she already felt for him had flowered into something so wonderful that it was nearly unbearable. But in a few days she would be just a stray from South America, and she would have to watch while Luke went off with the woman he loved, and who loved him. Janna had no illusions about his lovemaking. For her it had been wonderful. For him? A physical need satisfied, that was all. She had read enough books to know the ways of men, to know that however much he had seemed to need her, to want her, it had been a purely physical reaction on his part. She would never know why she had taunted him beyond endurance as she had, until he had taken her, possessed her with a fierce, deep anger that had been painful and wonderful at the same time. The awful thing was—she knew she would do it again, if she had to. And that should have filled her with shame, but it didn't. She'll have him for the rest of their lives, she thought. I'll have him for only a few days more. It wasn't too much to ask.

She picked up her bag, and Luke followed her out, and they went down, both hungry, to see if there was any belated breakfast.

After a late lunch that afternoon, Luke told Janna and Eva that he was going out on business, and would be back before dinner. Janna watched him drive off in the Land Rover and then went back to rejoin Eva by the pool. It was an extremely hot, humid day, and Eva had given her a brand new bikini that, she said, 'didn't suit her'. Janna wondered if it were the truth, or if Eva found it a tactful way to make a gift without offending her. She had never worn one before, and twirled round in front of her bedroom mirror, delighted at the look of it. Two strips of black silk, as brief as brief could be, and the effect was quite interesting.

Luke had come in as she was admiring herself, and gave a low whistle.

'*Very* nice,' he said. Janna drew herself up to her

full height, pleasantly aware that his eyes were riveted on her slender figure. They weren't in England yet. Here, he was hers—just briefly.

'I didn't know they existed,' she said.

'You've a lot to learn,' he remarked, amused.

'Why do you have to go out?' she asked.

'I'm going to call in at our place, as we're so near.'

'Oh, I see.' She crossed the room to him and reached up to put her arms round his neck, and kissed him.

He held her arms gently, smiling. 'What was that for?' he asked.

'Nothing. Just—thank you for finding me.' Her eyes shone.

He sighed. 'Dear child, don't thank me—you have no need.'

'But I do!'

He disengaged her arms gently from round his neck and held them loosely. 'You're so young,' he said. 'So very young, and innocent—and I took that away from you. When you thank me like that, it makes me feel like an absolute swine. I'll help you as much as I can to find your family, Janna, because I wouldn't feel happy if I didn't—but please don't thank me.'

'I wanted it as much as you,' she whispered. 'I'm a woman, not a child. I know, when we go back to England, it'll be over, but while we're here, tonight and tomorrow—and until we go, let me—let us——'

'You don't know what you're saying,' he said, his voice shaken.

'I do. I've thought about it, and I do,' she whispered. 'I know you belong to Annabel—I *know* that, and it's all right, but while we're here, let this time

be ours.' Her grey eyes met and held his, and she
saw his change and darken, and knew by the ting-
ling at the back of her neck, and down her spine,
that his need for her—whether purely physical or
not—was great. She slid her arms round his waist
and leaned her head against his chest, and heard the
quickening beat of his heart. He put his arms
around her, slowly, almost reluctantly, and she felt
his deep breath in a sigh in his chest. She looked up
at him, standing on tiptoe, fragile and vulnerable
against his great strength—saw his face, nearer,
nearer, then felt his warm sensual lips come over
hers.

Without any haste, he reached up and unfastened
the flimsy strip of black silk, and it fluttered to the
floor. 'This is madness,' he whispered. 'Utter madness.'

'I know,' she whispered in return, and slid against
him. 'Teach me, that's all I want, teach me——'

His lips found her pulse at her throat. 'You don't
need teaching anything,' he murmured, and his
hands slid down her body, then he picked her up, as
light as a feather, no effort needed, and took her to
the bed and lay down with her.

She undid the buttons on his shirt, one by one by
one, teasing his chest with her fingers as she did so,
touching, teasing, gently pulling the dark hairs that
covered him, until he groaned and begged her to
stop or he would punish her, so she did it all the
more, and asked him what the punishment would
be, then, slowly and lingeringly, he told her . . . and
showed her. . . .

Afterwards, when she had waved him off and
gone to rejoin Eva, she remembered, and was warm
with the memories. Eva smiled at her and then
laughed, a deep throaty laugh.

'Why are you laughing?' asked Janna, and joined in helplessly.

'Because—just because!' Eva answered. 'You remind me of *me* many years ago, when Luis and I were first married. Ah!' she sighed. 'But that is enough, or I will embarrass you.' She chuckled. 'We must have some champagne, I think.' She lifted a bell by her chair and shook it until the sounds tinkled and reverberated round the pond.

'You were very kind to ask us to stay,' said Janna. 'I can't thank you enough.'

'The pleasure is ours. You are always welcome here. You must come again, whenever you are near Rio d'Oro. There is always a place for you and Luke, always.'

But she wouldn't be here again. And if he came, it would be with Annabel. Janna gave herself a little mental shake. Now was now—and now was the time she had, and it was what mattered. 'Thank you,' she said.

Eva began to talk about the party, then they sipped icy cold champagne, and had a swim, and when Eva's youngest son arrived he joined them, a handsome serious-faced boy with exquisite manners, who asked his mother if he might sit with them before doing so.

The time passed pleasantly, then Luis arrived home and Eva went off to see about dinner, while Janna began to wonder where Luke had got to.

They were dressed and drinking in the *salón* when he returned, and Janna could see by his face as soon as he came in that something had happened. She was aware that she was keenly attuned to all his moods, almost as if she were a part of him. She didn't question this, she accepted it as she did her love for him. It didn't matter that he didn't love her, and regarded her as a child—most of the time anyway, she thought, with a secret smile—she loved him and she wanted only to see him happy. But something was wrong. She knew it as if he had spoken. Eva and Luis clearly noticed nothing. They welcomed him warmly back, and Luis gave him a whisky, and soon afterwards they went in to dinner, and Luke was his usual self—but Janna knew different.

It was not until midnight, and they were alone, that she found out what was the matter. She locked their bedroom door and went over to him. 'What is it, Luke?' she asked. 'Can you tell me?'

He looked down at her and smiled reluctantly. 'What do you mean?'

'I knew the minute you came back that something was wrong. If it's private, just say so, I won't pry—but I know you've had a shock.'

'You're very astute,' he commented.

Only because I love you, she thought. Your unhappiness is mine—but she didn't say it. 'I know,' she smiled.

'I'll tell you.' He touched her cheek, stroked it with his finger. 'It'll please you, actually.'

She shook her head. 'Not if it makes you unhappy. How can it?'

'Ah, but this will.' He motioned towards the bed. 'Let's sit down—hell, I could do with a drink!'

'So could I,' she said.

He stood up. 'I'm going down. Stay there.'

He was back within minutes with a bottle of champagne and two glasses. He opened it and poured a full glass each, while Janna looked at him, puzzled and apprehensive. How on earth could something that upset him please her?

She drank long and deep, to give her the courage

to hear. He sat down beside her. 'I drove over to our factory today,' he said.

'I know.'

'I had a look round, then I went into the office for a talk with the head man there.' He paused and drank some champagne. 'He told me some news—that shattered me.' She caught her breath.

'Go on.'

'I was telling him that I intended going shortly to the Sierra Alta—where Cordilla lives—and it turned out that he knows him. I hadn't mentioned Cordilla's name, you understand, I was merely sounding him out about the area—it was he who mentioned him first. He told me——' he twisted the glass round by its stem, 'there'd been a disaster there recently, a landslide, that had trapped twenty cars on a narrow country road for hours until they could be dug out.' He looked at her. 'Several people were injured. The worst was——' he paused.

'Cordilla?' she whispered.

'Yes. He's paralysed. It's doubtful if he'll live. He'll certainly never walk again.'

Janna was shaken. 'How dreadful!' she said. Then she looked up. 'B-but how could you think that *that* would please me?'

'I didn't mean in that sense—I'm sorry. But don't you see? It's finished now.'

'The—stamp?'

'Yes. I'm not going there now. To take a stamp that he's stolen off an able-bodied man is one thing, but to go and rob an invalid, someone who's paralysed——' he shook his head. 'No.'

'You mean—when we leave on Wednesday——' she stopped, heart in mouth.

'I mean I won't be returning. Yes. I've left my

Land Rover at the plant. Davis—the boss—will sell it for me. He dropped me back here.'

Janna let out a deep, deep sigh. She finished her glass and got up to pour some more. Holding out the bottle, she asked: 'Some more for you?'

'Please.' She filled both glasses and sat down again.

'And you never knew before?'

'No.'

'If you had—found out—you'd never have reached Santa Cruz, would you.'

'No.'

She let her breath out in a long deep sigh. 'Phew!'

Luke laughed. 'Is that all you can say?'

'For the moment—yes. I'm glad you won't be coming back, not for that anyway.' She put her hand on his arm. 'I'm sorry about everything else, though. I mean, you'd set your heart on it——'

'It's over now. Finished.' He gave a wry smile. 'I don't cry over spilt milk. And I never look back. There's you to see to now. Home—and the search.'

'Yes,' she said, and finished her drink. She got up to put her glass on the table, then took his from him. 'I'm tired, Luke. Can we go to bed?'

'That's what we came for.' He unfastened his tie and pulled it off, then stood up. 'I'm going to have a shower. Unless you want one first?' He was unfastening his shirt as he spoke, and she went forward to help him, and looked up at him as she eased it over the bandage. 'There's a water shortage,' she said gravely. 'I forgot to tell you. We've been asked to save water.'

He looked at her, stunned, then light dawned, and he started to laugh. 'Really?'

'Mmm,' she nodded. Then, very slowly, she lifted

her dress and eased it over her head. She looked
steadily at him as she took off her clothes, and he
didn't look away, he stood very still, watching her.
When she had finished she went forward and un-
buckled his belt. 'Your arm's sore,' she whispered.
'You need help.'

'Yes, I suppose I do,' he answered. His face had
gone very serious, and he stood there as Janna
helped him, then she took his hand and led him, like
a child, into the shower cubicle.

The water, lukewarm, sprayed out, and she began
to soap him gently, making him hold his bandaged
arm out of the way. 'I'll do that later,' she whispered. He nodded. His eyes had a glazed look, as if
he didn't quite know what was happening, and she
washed him, then herself, and led him out again and
switched the water off, and picked up a towel and
knelt to dry his feet. Then she dried her own.
Taking his hand, she led him into the bedroom and
began to smooth the towel over him until he was
dry. Luke looked down at her, and she saw in his
eyes what she already knew, and she handed him
the towel.

'Please—dry me,' she whispered, and smiled at
him. He began to rub her very, very gently, dabbing
and patting, and pausing, then going on. After a few
minutes, when it was now very evident that he
wanted her, he said:

'Janna, this is wrong—so very wrong——' and
the towel slithered silently to the carpet as he
reached for her, almost as if his arms were moving
without his volition. His hands belied his words.
'This is madness——'

'Yes, I know.' She arched her body so that they
touched, and all was fire.

His hands had a fine tremor to them as he

caressed her dry skin. 'Dear God, I want you so much,' he whispered brokenly, 'but don't you realise the danger——' He buried his face in her damp, sweet-smelling hair, and his voice was muffled.

'Danger?' she whispered. 'To be—together?' She trembled. 'Just for a short time, that's all, after—when we reach England—no more. Is it too much to ask, now, here?'

'Not that—if that were all,' he groaned. 'I could give you a child—and you're little more than one——' He couldn't speak further. Janna sensed his anguish, and her love for him flared up into a wild flame. His child—to have his child—how wonderful that would be! She clung to him and moaned his name, softly, over and over, softly—gently, and, as if he could not help himself, Luke picked her up in his arms and carried her across to the bed.

CHAPTER SEVEN

JANNA felt no shame. How could she when she loved him with all her heart? She lay cradled in his arms and slept, blissfully unaware that through that long night Luke slept but little, and that, tormented. Had she known, had she woken, she would have soothed him, but their lovemaking had been so profound, so deep, that her sleep was one of utter exhaustion. The hours passed, and she woke to see him looking at her, as if imprinting every inch of her on his mind. She smiled sleepily at him and gave a deep contented purr. 'Hello,' she whispered. 'I didn't know you were awake. Why didn't you wake me?'

'You need your sleep,' he said, and traced the outline of her smooth face with his finger. 'I've hardly slept at all.'

'Oh no!' She was distressed. 'I'm sorry, Luke—do you want me to rub your back? That will make you sleepy. Have you got a headache?'

'No, there's nothing you can do.' She felt ashamed that she had been so blissfully unaware of his inability to sleep. Was it her fault? She reached up to touch his cheek, smoothing it gently.

'Poor Luke,' she said. 'Poor, poor Luke——' It was still dark, probably four or five, no later, and she had an idea. 'Let me pour you some champagne.' She giggled. 'That might knock you out.'

He sighed. 'No, it won't. Go to sleep. I'll close my eyes and relax.'

'All right.' She snuggled up to him, warm flesh against warm flesh, and idly, almost without thinking about it, ran her hand along the hard muscular skin of his body. She loved to touch him. She loved everything about him. 'Mmm, you're beautifully built,' she murmured. 'So strong—You're very strong, aren't you?'

'Yes. Go to sleep—please,' he said, and his voice had a faintly desperate note.

'Don't you like me stroking you?'

There was a full pause. Then: 'What do you think?' he said huskily.

'I don't know. That's why I'm asking,' she said, bewildered.

She heard him swallow—with some difficulty, it seemed to her. 'Of course I like it,' he said. 'Too much—so please stop.'

'Oh.' The meaning of his words sank in, and she giggled softly and renewed her attack, but Luke grabbed her hand and held it.

'I said—please—no!' His grip was like a vice. She wriggled her fingers against him and he brought his hand up—and hers—and bit her finger, not hard, but not gently either.

'Oh—ouch!' she exclaimed, and, easing herself up slightly, pinched him hard on his side. 'Take that! You're a beast!'

He turned over and imprisoned her with his leg, and pinched her in return. The next second they were struggling violently under the bedclothes, she pummelling him, he seeking to restrain her—and then, inflamed by the violent physical contact, and as she began to call him names, he silenced her most effectively with his mouth, and she yielded her lips to him, and closed her eyes, and allowed the sweet gentle movements of love to take over. . . .

They caught a plane to Rio on Wednesday morning, and from there flew to England. It was Thursday afternoon when they arrived at Heathrow, and Luke smiled at her as she gazed round in wonder, eyes wide. She couldn't believe that she was really here at last. 'Pinch me,' she said. 'I'm dreaming, aren't I?' They were in the restaurant.

'No, you're really here, in England, Janna. I thought we might stay a night or so in London before going home. No one knows we're here, and I thought it would be nice for you to look round London before I take you to my mother's.'

'That would be lovely.' She took a deep breath of the warm London air. 'I just want to do anything that suits you.' Her face radiated her happiness and the sheer joy of being alive, and she saw his eyes on her, dark, deep unfathomable. She thought she knew the meaning of his look, and touched his arm. 'It's all right,' she said softly. 'I know—that when we get to your house—it's finished. I know that, I won't let you down—ever, Luke. Please believe me.'

'I know,' he answered, equally quietly, and looked away, and she thought she saw pain in his eyes. She hoped that he believed her. She would never do anything to hurt him—surely he must know that? But perhaps he didn't. He had saved her, brought her safely here, and as well as her love, he had her heartfelt gratitude. He loved Annabel, and that was all right. She had never really imagined, only in her dreams, and they were secret, that she could ever share his life, but at least she had the memory of a week that she would never forget as long as she lived. She had more richness to remember than many people had in a lifetime.

'Please don't look like that,' she said. 'You mustn't be unhappy. How can you be? You're back in England, soon you'll see Annabel. Is it the stamp that's bothering you?'

Luke looked at her across the table and smiled wryly. 'I'd practically forgotten about that,' he sighed. 'I told you, I never look back.'

'Oh, I do! I'll always remember this last week— we could hardly have crammed much more into it, could we?' Janna bit her lip. 'I mean, leaving the café—the Mission—travelling to Rio d'Oro, staying at Eva and Luis's——'

'I know,' he said. He looked tired. 'Drink your coffee and we'll get a taxi.'

'Luke,' she said. He looked up from the packet of cigarettes he was opening.

'Yes?'

'It's all over now, isn't it? When we stay at this hotel, until we go to your house. Are we going to be registered separately?'

'I think it better, don't you?'

'Do you want an honest answer? Or do you want me to agree with you?' she smiled. 'It's all right, I'm only joking. I knew, once we were here, it—was finished. I just thought, when you said we'd be staying here——' She grinned impishly. 'I thought— Whoopee! an extra couple of days!'

Luke smiled. 'You're a shameless little hussy, you know that?'

'Yes,' she nodded, and he laughed and put his hand on hers.

'You're also refreshingly honest. I've never met anyone like you.'

'I wasn't honest when we met. Remember?' She pulled a face. 'Pretending to be a boy——'

'That was different. It was a necessary lie, as you saw it. I mean in other things. No guile, no subtlety——'

'Should I have?'

He shrugged. 'Sometimes, in life, it helps to hide your true feelings. You learn not to get hurt that way.'

Then he was wrong, because she was clearly managing to hide her true feelings for him. Perhaps she was learning. 'I can't imagine you letting anything hurt you,' she said gently. 'You're very tough.'

'Am I?' He played with a match. 'Perhaps I am. Finished your coffee?'

'Yes. I can't wait to walk down a *real* London street. Imagine!'

He took her arm and guided her through the crowded airport concourse, with the flight arrivals and departures being announced in high, clear, metallic tones, and the bustle and excitement of people on their journeys coming over in waves.

The taxi drove them away, their luggage in the boot, and after a circuitous journey through rush hour traffic, deposited them at a quiet hotel in a shady, tree-lined square away from the main city noise.

Janna stood in her room and looked out of the window. A telegram boy puttered past on a motor-scooter, and a pigeon landed on her windowsill and looked at her with beady eye. Luke had the room next to hers, and they shared a bathroom. The hotel was old-fashioned with an atmosphere of ordered elegance and no hurry. Janna's own images of London had been coloured by books she had read, and this was just how she imagined a hotel would have been in Victorian times. She told Luke so when he came in a moment or two later, and he laughed.

'You're quite right,' he said. 'My father used to stay here sometimes. He said it was the only place where they never seemed in a hurry—and you get heavenly breakfasts—just wait and see. It wouldn't do for someone in a mad dash, but for us, for you, to adjust to a different type of living, it's ideal.'

'You're spending so much money,' she protested, dismayed. 'I feel—so helpless—but one day, I pro-mise, I'll find a way to repay you.'

'You're going to become rich—a tycoon, perhaps? Or marry a millionaire?' he teased her.

'I'm not joking! You'll see.' She had no idea what work she would do. And she would have to find a job. Even if she traced relatives, she would be inde-pendent, because that was the way she had been brought up, to think for herself, to use her mind to its fullest capacity. She lifted her chin proudly. 'You'll see.'

'I think I will,' he said quietly. 'You're a very strong character, Janna—You'll land on your feet, whatever you choose to do.'

She traced a pattern on the glass, an aimless squiggle, and grinned at him. 'Can we go a walk before dinner, please?'

'Of course. That's what I came to ask you. Aren't you tired?'

'No. I slept on the plane. Didn't you?'

'No. We're supposed to be suffering from jet lag.'

'What on earth's that?'

Luke stared at her and shook his head. 'If you don't know, you've obviously not got it. Come on.' He took her arm. He seemed bemused.

They spent two hours walking round London— Oxford Street, window-gazing, the quieter back streets, and Janna was enthralled, totally bewildered by the crowds of people, the traffic—it was difficult for her to get used to that, plus the fact that, as far as she was concerned, everybody drove on the wrong side. She was not aware of Luke's eyes on her so many times, as she gazed in wonder at some landmark of which she had only seen photographs, and which she was now seeing in the flesh, as it were.

They had dinner at the hotel, and afterwards she felt a sudden wave of exhaustion sweep over her. Luke looked at her, saw her white face, and said, 'Bed for you.'

She nodded. 'I think so. What about you?'

'I'll have a drink in the bar, then make a few phone calls—you don't mind, do you?'

'Of course not. I'll go up.' She looked longingly at the glass doors into the T.V. lounge. She had never seen television before. That, too, was unbelievable. But there was time, plenty of time. . . .

'Goodnight, Luke.'

'Goodnight, Janna.' She walked away, tall and proud, and he watched her go.

The next thing she knew was that someone was shaking her arm and telling her that it was time she got up. She opened her eyes to see Luke, fully dressed in slim-fitting grey trousers and black shirt, looking down at her.

Janna rubbed her eyes and sat up slowly, gazing in utter puzzlement at him.

'It's Friday morning, it's nine-fifteen, and they stop serving breakfast at nine-thirty,' he said gently.

She took a deep breath. 'Ooh, I'd better get——'

'Um, you better had. And hurry, I'm starving.' He stood up and went out. 'I'll be downstairs in the lounge reading the paper. You've got *five* minutes.'

'Yes, *sir*!' She scrambled out of bed as he went out. A cold wash was all she had time for, but it did the trick, and five minutes later she was running downstairs, dressed in a simple but chic yellow sundress that had cost a small fortune in Rio d'Oro. Luke was reading a morning paper and she went over and tapped his arm. 'Come on, slowcoach,' she said. 'I want my breakfast and all you can do is sit there reading!' He lifted his hand as if to strike her, his eyes glinting with humour, and stood up. An elderly colonel looked up from the *Guardian* and went 'Humph' and Luke muttered:

'Think yourself lucky he was here.'

'Hah!' she whispered back, as quietly, as they left the colonel to his crossword. 'You don't scare *me*!'

He took her arm as they went into the breakfast

room, which was nearly empty. My first English breakfast, Janna thought. She had visions of maids in black dresses and stiff starched white aprons, and toast and marmalade and huge cups of tea. That seemed to be what they ate in the books she had read—and the reality was almost the same, but there was so much more besides. Bacon and eggs and teeny grilled mushrooms with the crisp portions of fried bread, and sausage and tomatoes. She tucked into it all with gusto, watched by an astonished Luke, who ate his own breakfast slowly, spending more time observing her delight.

'Oh dear,' she sighed, replete at last. 'I can't *move*!'

'Good grief, I thought you were never going to stop,' he said, and added drily: 'Want this bacon?'

'Heavens, no. That's yours.' She looked round at the oak-panelled room. An elderly couple were about to depart, the woman collecting her bag, the man fussing round her, taking her arm. They bowed slightly as they went out, murmured: 'Good morning,' and beamed politely.

'Good morning,' Luke and Janna echoed.

They looked at each other and smiled. 'Drink your tea,' said Luke. 'We're going out. Harrods first, then lunch at the Ritz.'

'Wow! Really?'

'Really.'

'And then?'

He shrugged. 'We'll see. A walk round Soho, perhaps.'

'What's there?' she frowned, and he laughed.

'You'll see.'

She finished her tea, and they went out, into a warm summer's day.

It was the start of an action-filled day, one which
lasted until nearly eleven, when, both tired, they
returned to their hotel. Janna practically fell into
bed, and was asleep almost immediately. Luke had
told her they would be returning to his home in
Surrey on the Sunday morning. They would have
one more day in London, one full day together, and
then she would meet his mother, and be a guest at
his house, and the work of tracing any relatives she
might have would begin.

One more day, she thought, just before sleep
claimed her. We must make the most of that. . . .

And they did. They strolled past Buckingham
Palace, along with a few hundred others, had a boat
ride on the Thames, visited Westminster Abbey, had
a meal at a small Italian restaurant where the food
was delicious, and went to a pub for a drink before
returning to their hotel at ten.

'I've had the most lovely day of my life,' said
Janna, as they walked up the stairs to their rooms.
'Truly, it's been marvellous. Thank you so much,
Luke.'

He took her key from her and opened her door,
and they went in. 'I've enjoyed it too,' he said. 'You
know, it's odd, isn't it? I've lived here all my life—
and yet seeing everything through your eyes was like
seeing a new city.' He sat on the bed and groaned.
'My feet are killing me!'

She began to laugh. 'Poor thing! *Mine* aren't. I
could walk *miles*!'

'I'm older than you,' he reminded her gently, and
his expression was rather strange, and she
caught her breath. She shouldn't have said it. She
didn't want the happy mood shattered. She knelt at
his feet and eased his shoes off and began to rub

them, and he laughed and caught her hand. 'Stop!' he exclaimed.

'Why?'

'I'm ticklish, you idiot!'

She laughed too, at that, and renewed her attack. 'I said *stop* it!' he protested, gritting his teeth, and he pulled her hands away and held them, and growled ferociously at her.

'All right,' she said. 'Let me go—I won't do it again, honest!'

At least the strange look, the one she hadn't understood, had gone. Luke let go of her hands and she rose slowly to her feet and sat beside him on the bed. Then she sighed, a soft, sad sigh. 'I'll remember this day as long as I live,' she said.

He didn't answer, and she thought that he hadn't heard. She looked at him, and saw what was on his face, and her heart thudded. She put her hand on his. 'What is it?' she asked, fearful. 'Please——'

He shook his head. 'Nothing, Janna.' He looked at her.

'Are you angry at me for saying that?' she whispered.

'No!' He laid his hand on her cheek. 'It was a very nice thing to say. How could I be angry?'

She looked deep into his eyes, grey eyes, deep, dark grey, and her own were wide and bright. I love you, she thought, and it was like a poem in her heart, one that could never be spoken. She wondered if the love showed on her face, and if it did, it didn't matter. She closed her eyes and nuzzled her face into his hand, her lips touching lightly against his palm.

She felt his other hand come up, and touch her hair, and he stroked it carefully and gently, then took her in his arms. She opened her mouth to his, and it was a sweet tender kiss, a kiss full of longing and unspoken dreams, and infinitely sad.

Luke moved slightly away, looked at her, and his face was softer and gentler than ever she had seen it. 'Dear Janna,' he whispered. 'You're such an innocent child——'

'I'm a woman,' she murmured, and put her soft warm hand round the back of his neck and caressed it with her fingers. She ached with longing for him, a sweet desire for him to make love to her, and she knew, with her sure feminine instinct, that he wanted her. But they were in England now, and the brief marriage was over. She had taken her ring off and wore it with the cross at her breast, where it was warm and safe. She put her hand on her dress, to reassure herself that it was there, and he covered her hand with his own, stroking it very gently.

'Don't leave me yet,' she whispered. 'Stay a while.'

'I mustn't,' he answered. 'We both know why.'

'No, nothing—just to hold me, that's all I ask— just hold me.'

'Dear girl,' he said softly, 'if I held you in my arms it wouldn't end there, and we both know that.' He gave a deep sigh.

'Would it be so wrong?' she murmured.

'Yes.' He moved his hand from her breast, and lifted her chin and smiled at her. 'Yes, it would.'

'Then——' her voice was shaky, 'I think you'd better go.'

'I know.' He stood up and pulled her to her feet, and kissed her on her forehead. His hands on her arms had a fine tremor, and she leaned against him and began to cry softly.

'Don't——' he began.

'It's—all right,' she managed, through muffled sobs, 'honestly, I'm just—it's been so wonderful, today, and yesterday—so wonderful——' She raised tear-stained cheeks to him. 'Today,' she whispered, 'I've never been so happy in my life. And I'll always be grateful to you.'

'Please don't—I've told you——' He shook his head, anguished.

She made a great effort and pushed him away, turned from him, and went over to the window. Taking a deep breath, she asked: 'How are we travelling to your home tomorrow?' She wiped her cheeks furtively, sniffed once, and remained standing with her back to him.

'By taxi,' he said, only his voice was nearer than it had been, and he was behind her, standing, not touching, but close. 'We'll leave here about eleven.'

'That will be nice,' she answered. 'I'm looking forward to it.'

'Turn round, Janna,' he said.

'No-o, I want to look out of the window. It's lovely, isn't it? All these trees—so quiet, so peaceful——'

'Janna,' he said again, 'turn round,' and he put his arms on her to move her round to face him, and then she was.

She blinked, gave him a lovely smile, and said, very brightly: 'Don't you like the view——' She faltered, seeing his expression. She was keeping herself rigidly under control, and he mustn't make it difficult like that. 'The—the trees——'

'Yes,' he said, 'I do. Oh yes——' His arms moved as if of their own volition, and slid round her. 'Very much. From where I'm standing.' But he wasn't looking out of the window, he was looking at her, and he moved closer to her so that their bodies were

touching, and she could feel the beat of his heart as
he held her, feel the hard length of his body against
hers, then he reached for the zip at the back of her
dress and slid it slowly down, and the dress slithered
to the floor.

'Very much,' he said again, and she stepped out
of the dress as he took her hand in his and led her to
the bed. She lay back and took him into her waiting
arms, and he kissed her again deeply, arousing her
to a pitch of excitement with the warm movements
of his hands, then he reached up and pulled the
light cord, and the room was in darkness, and for a
few minutes the only sounds heard were the soft
whisper of clothes as they were removed.

Warmth filled her, a tide of rushing warmth, but
there was no haste, no hurry, just the limbs that
touched, the hands that caressed and teased, the
mouths that met and clung in the rising tide of excitement and passion such as she had never known
before—and knew she never would again.

CHAPTER EIGHT

Luke had telephoned his mother on Sunday
morning before their departure. He looked now at
Janna as the taxi drove along a quiet country lane.
'We're nearly there,' he told her. 'My mother will
be at church when we arrive, but I'll show you
round.'

They had spoken little over breakfast. Janna was
faintly apprehensive about what was going to
happen, and had a sadness within her at what was

passed and gone. It was like the beginning of a new era in her life. She couldn't tell him—he wouldn't understand. No one could. She was alone, in a sense, not belonging anywhere, or to anyone. She might or might not trace relatives, but whatever happened, she would learn to be independent in this new country to which Luke had brought her. Life with her father, although happy, had not been easy. He had few possessions, and had worked among the Indians and people around Santa Cruz for virtually nothing, seeking no reward, it seemed, receiving more often than not food or trinkets in exchange for his services. Never once had he seemed discontent. It was as though he had devoted his life to others. Janna had never been hungry, or lacking in affection, but her life had been one of spartan simplicity, and she had known no other way of life, and she had been happy.

But within days she had been catapulted into another world; the opulence of wealthy living in Rio d'Oro; the plane flight from there to an unknown country—and now, going to the house of this man whom she loved and to whom she owed more than her life. He seemed withdrawn, and she sensed it was because he was returning to his loved ones, and perhaps wondered if she would fit in. She wondered if he also regretted being unfaithful to Annabel, but it was something she could never ask. She also wondered if he was apprehensive about her telling the woman he loved. He need have no fear, she thought, looking at him, sitting beside her, silent, unsmiling—and he would soon be reassured about that. She sighed, and he turned and looked at her.

'There's my house,' he said. 'Nearly home.'

Janna looked, and saw they were approaching a

large sprawling house of mellow red brick, with ivy spreading along its walls. There were high chimneys, and it was surrounded by trees.

The driver slowed and turned into the drive, which curved round gently until they reached the front. Janna looked at it as she climbed out, and saw the large windows, blank and shiny in the sunlight, and smoke curling from one of the chimneys.

A black labrador rushed towards them, barking, and Luke grabbed his collar as the taxi turned to drive away, then released him. The dog jumped up whining ecstatically, tail wagging, and Luke laughed and said, 'This is Nero. Say hello to Janna.'

The dog spared her a brief glance before resuming his frenzied greeting and Luke picked up their cases, added, 'Get down, you fool!' and turned to Janna. 'Come on,' he said.

The front door was unlocked and he led her into a wide, warm hall, with dark panelled walls and a red carpet, and several half-open doors leading off. Luke put down the cases, and a small woman appeared, wiping her hands on her apron. She was elderly, clad in black, and she was smiling.

'Welcome home, Luke,' she said. 'It's good to see you back.'

'Hello, Matty,' he hugged her. 'Mother not back yet?'

'No, but she'll not be long. Said to tell you she was calling on old Mrs Frobisher on her way home.' She smiled at Janna.

'This is Matty, Janna,' he said. 'Mainstay of the house. Keep on the right side of her and you'll be all right.' He grinned at the woman, who tutted as if shocked and tapped his arm.

'I don't know what people will think,' she said,

rosy-cheeked. 'How d'you do, miss. Take no notice of him. I'm pleased to meet you.'

They shook hands. Janna realised that the woman was probably over seventy, but with young eyes in a lined face. 'Hello, Matty,' she said. 'Is it all right to call you that?'

'Bless you, everyone else does. Who'd have a name like Matilda, anyway?' she snorted. 'Come on in the kitchen. The kettle's on and I've just made some of your favourite scones.'

'Sounds fine, lead the way.'

The kitchen was large, ultra-modern, white and blue. Janna had never seen anything like it in her life, and looked round in wonder. Luke watched her, as did the woman, who seemed puzzled by something.

'Sit down, do,' she said. 'And don't get in my way for a moment.' This with a wink at Janna as Luke obediently sat. Nero, who had followed them in, was shooed out, and Matty produced a plate of scones, still warm, and a butter dish. 'Now you get buttering,' she said. 'And no more than two each or you won't eat your lunch.'

She bustled about, filling a teapot, and Luke grinned at Janna across the table and handed her a buttered scone. 'She thinks she can still boss me about, you know, and she's no more than a shrimp——' He ducked as Matty aimed a clip at his ear. 'Sorry, Matty, only joking.'

She sniffed, mouth quivering. 'Time was, *you* were no bigger than a shrimp yourself,' she said. 'And you were just as cheeky then.' She poured out three cups of tea, and sat down with them. 'So you're back home, are you? To stay a while, I hope?'

'Probably.' He bit into a scone. 'Mmm, well up

to standard.' He flicked some butter from his chin.
'I missed these while I was roaming South America.'
He looked at the little woman, his face softening.
'There's nothing like your home cooking, my dear,
no matter where I go. I'll always be back.' He
looked at Janna. 'Matty's been with us since I was a
baby. She's family, aren't you, love?' He reached
out to grasp the wrinkled hand on the table, and the
woman nodded, eyes filled with warmth as she
looked at him.

'Aye, that I have,' she said. 'Are you going to tell
me who Janna is?'

Luke looked at Janna, then began speaking. He
told her the whole story, from the beginning, in the
bar, and Janna listened, and it was like hearing
about someone else. The only thing he never mentioned was the wedding, naturally enough. Matty
listened in utter silence, and when he had done, she
had tears in her eyes.

'Oh my,' she said. 'Oh my! And you're going to
help her find her own folks?'

'I'm going to try,' he said quietly. 'And until we
do, this will be her home.'

She sighed. 'Of course, of course. I hope you do,
me dear. It's like a fairy tale, isn't it?' She blinked,
as if aware that she was being foolish, and drank her
tea. Then she stood up and removed the plate of
scones. 'Have you told your mother?' she asked Luke.

'Not yet. There wasn't time on the phone. You're
the first to hear.'

Matty regarded Janna, her face setting into a
smile. 'You were a lucky girl,' she said. 'Very lucky.
If anyone can help you, it's Luke.'

'I know.' Janna smiled back at her. In the distance the dog began to bark, and a door closed.

'Here she is,' said Matty.

The next moment the door to the kitchen opened, a voice said: 'Matty, have they——' and stopped. Janna turned slowly as Luke got up, and she saw him stride over towards the woman standing in the doorway, and hug her. 'Darling! You're home!' she exclaimed, and looked towards Janna, and then smiled. Janna stood up, shy and unsure of herself. Luke's mother was tall and slim, dressed elegantly in a grey tweed suit and silk blouse, dark hair speckled with grey, swept back into a chignon, and with a beautiful face, an older, feminine version of Luke.

'Hello. You're Janna,' she said, and came forward to take her hand. 'Welcome to England.'

'Thank you, Mrs Hayes-Ross,' said Janna, and thought suddenly: This is my mother-in-law, and it's *my* name as well. It was a very strange sensation. Luke's mother looked at her steadily, out of the same grey eyes as her son's, and Janna had the uncomfortable feeling that the older woman could read into her mind, was as shrewd, possibly shrewder, than he.

Matty said, 'Lunch will be ready in half an hour—and we're having it in here today. My rheumatism's playing me up and I'm not traipsing into that dining room.'

His mother laughed. 'All right, Matty. We'll go and have a drink in the drawing-room.'

She turned and led the way out, and Janna and Luke followed. She led them into a large comfortable room where a log fire burned in the fireplace, and Mrs Hayes-Ross sat down on a long settee and patted the cushion beside her. 'Sit down, Janna. Luke will get the drinks. Martini for me, dear.' She smiled at Janna. 'Now,' she said, 'tell me how you met Luke.'

Janna froze, panicking. This woman was so different from the kindly housekeeper. She was elegant, assured, and she was clearly wondering what this little waif was doing in her home, for which Janna didn't blame her. She knew that she was from another world than this. It was like a test. To fail it would be to let Luke down, and she wasn't under any circumstances going to do that.

'I've lived all my life near a small town in Peru,' she said steadily. She wasn't ashamed of her background. Why should she be? She might be poor, but she had had a father of whom she was proud, and whom she had loved deeply, and this woman, living her life of ordered elegance, couldn't ever begin to know or imagine the kind of people who had been her father's patients. Janna sensed, not that she was hostile, not that, but that she had reservations about this young stranger who had come abruptly into her home. That was fair enough, too. Luke was in the background, and there was the chink of bottles and glasses, but he seemed to be taking his time, perhaps for a reason.

Janna lifted her head proudly. She wasn't going to let him down either—but particularly, she was not going to let herself down. If Luke's mother made it clear that she didn't want her to stay, she would leave. But first she would tell her story, as she had been asked. She looked straight and steady into the eyes of the waiting woman, then began to tell her of her father's sudden death from a heart attack, all those weeks ago, and then, very briefly of the work he had done for years there, and of how he had been liked and respected by all with whom he came into contact. She had never even told Luke all these things. She was aware that he had gone very still, and was listening, and as the pictures flooded back to her, and she spoke quietly but firmly, painting for the two listeners the images as best she knew how, her confidence grew. She was her father's daughter. The love, and the pride, shone through in her quietly spoken words, and the atmosphere changed, and Luke's mother was very still and serious, while Luke himself, when she looked up once, briefly, stood like a man in a dream.

The story progressed. In all it had taken many minutes to tell, and when Janna reached the point at which Luke had taken her to the Mission, she touched, quite unconsciously, the cross and the ring beneath her dress. She went on, about the journey and the shop in Rio d'Oro, and the flight to England. Then she said, at the finish, 'I would like to find my father's people—my people—if it's possible. It was suggested to me—and I suppose the thought was in my mind a long while before—that perhaps my father had done wrong, had gone to South America with my mother, under a different name. I'm prepared, for that knowledge—I only know, in my heart, that if he did whatever it was, he's paid for it many times over in the love and care he gave to so many poor people.'

She had finished. Tears were in her eyes, but she refused to blink them away. She looked proudly at Luke's mother and waited for what she would say, her head held high, her young face with a calm dignity to it, and saw that Luke was watching her as if he had never seen her before.

'My dear child,' said Mrs Hayes-Ross slowly, 'what a remarkable man your father was!' She smiled very gently at Janna. 'You have every right to be so proud of him. You will always have these memories to treasure.' And she reached out her hand and put it on Janna's. 'I'm glad you met my son, and that he brought you here. Very glad.'

The tears spilled over, and Janna sat there, her mouth quivering with spent emotion. 'Thank you,' she said. It was little more than a whisper.

Luke moved forward. He handed his mother a glass, and a handkerchief to Janna, 'Wipe those tears away,' he said, 'and drink this.'

She did so, then took a glass from him. Luke's mother sat very quietly sipping her Martini. The reservations had gone. Janna knew it without having to be told. The woman's poise was great, but she had been shaken by what she had heard. She stood up and put her glass on a table beside the settee. 'Do excuse me a moment,' she said, and went out.

Luke sat beside Janna. 'You never told me,' he said.

She looked at him. 'It wasn't necessary,' she answered.

He took a deep breath. 'But it was now?' he queried.

She nodded. 'Yes.'

'I see. You're quite right. But you knew that, didn't you?'

'Yes.'

'I was wrong. You're not a child, you're a mature woman.' He smiled faintly as he said it. 'You have a great sensitivity, Janna—and you're old, in some ways, beyond your years.'

'Only in some ways,' she answered, and tried to return his smile, but couldn't. She was still trembling with reaction. She bit her lip.

'I've not seen my mother so shaken in years,' he said, and touched her cheek gently.

'I didn't—I don't want to upset her,' she said.

'No, not that—but I watched her—I watched you both, while you were talking, and it was as though you were making her come awake, as though——' he hesitated, 'I don't know how to put it—I only know the effect you had on me.'

'And what was that?'

'You made me wish I'd met him,' he answered softly.

'You would have liked him. Please, don't make me cry again——'

'I'm sorry, I won't.' He smiled. 'I've done enough of that.' He looked at his watch. 'Nearly time to eat. Drink up!'

'You haven't had one,' she pointed out.

'So I haven't!' He stood up. 'But I didn't need one. Come on.'

His mother wasn't in the kitchen when they went out, but Matty had set four places at the large pine table, on brightly coloured mats, and she said, 'Sit down, you two. Where's your mother?'

'She'll be out in a moment,' Luke answered, and as he spoke, his mother came in.

They had a simple meal, clear soup followed by roast chicken, and fruit afterwards. It was delicious.

When it was over, Janna helped Matty to clear the dishes. It didn't occur to her not to, and when Luke said, 'You haven't come here to work,' she answered:

'Please let me.' She grinned at Matty. 'You don't mind, do you?'

'Not at all, me dear.'

Luke's mother said, with a look at her son: 'In that case, come and have a talk with me, dear. Tell me all about your adventures.'

The stamp, the original reason for Luke's journeying, hadn't yet been mentioned. She would want to hear about that. They went out, and Matty and Janna were alone.

'Let me make you a cup of tea, Matty,' said Janna. 'Sit down, and I'll get the washing up done.'

Matty laughed, but sat down. 'You wouldn't be feeling sorry for an old lady, would you?' she asked, blue eyes shrewdly resting on Janna's busy hands. Janna felt herself colour. She wouldn't have dreamed of saying so, but that was precisely what she had been doing. It seemed to her unfair that in a large, luxurious home like this, one old lady did all the work. While she was here, she would help her as much as possible.

'N-no, of course not,' she stammered. 'I just don't like being idle——'

'You're a kind child,' the old woman murmured. 'But you don't need to feel like that. Bless you, girl, I live a life of pampered luxury here,' and as Janna smiled—tactfully—hiding her disbelief, she hoped, the old woman added: 'Did you think I look after everything alone?'

Janna nodded, bit her lip, and Matty laughed. 'I thought so! Why, there's a housekeeper and two cleaning ladies come every day, me dear! But not on Sundays, d'you see? Sundays the kitchen is *mine*.'

'Oh, Matty!' Janna began to laugh, leaning on the sink by the bowl of soapy dish-filled water. 'You'll think me silly, won't you? I didn't realise! I thought——'

'You thought I was a poor old lady who had to work all the hours God sends to keep a big house like this going?' She shook her head. 'I'm retired— officially—but I've got no one in the world, so they told me, ten years ago, that this was my home for as long as I live, and so it's been. But I'm like you, I can't be idle, and I love cooking, so that's what I'll keep on doing for as long as I'm able. But every- thing's bought for me, every day, and bless you, dear, Sunday's the day when I'm queen of the kitchen. I do everything then.'

She sipped the tea that Janna had made, and sat back, contented. 'I've got my own room with all my little treasures, and a nice colour telly that Luke bought me, and my own bathroom—it's like a little palace—I'll show you later. Luke wouldn't take you there when he shows you round, not unless I said all right, because it's like my own little flat.' Her eyes shone. 'And Luke's the best of the lot—though you're not to say I said that—but he is. He's always been my favourite.'

And I love him too, thought Janna, but she couldn't say it. She put the last dish to drain and picked up her own cup, and sat at the table. 'He's been very kind to me,' she said. 'It would have taken me months to save any money—and then probably ages to get a passport—but he arranged everything within days. I'm very grateful to him.'

'I'm sure you are,' the old woman answered, looking at Janna very shrewdly.

'He's told me about his—fiancée,' said Janna, 'and she seems very nice.' The old lady was a mite too shrewd. It wouldn't do for her to guess Janna's secret.

'Miss Annabel? Aye, she is. She's a lovely girl. They're a fine couple together, well matched. Ever so sweet she is, always brings me a present when she's been on holiday.' She sighed. Janna listened in silence, the picture building up in her mind. What had she expected—or perhaps secretly hoped—to hear? That Annabel was a bitch? If so, she had been mistaken. She wished that she hadn't asked, but it was too late. The old woman chattered on about Annabel, and her love of horses, how she sometimes rode over on a Sunday—even when Luke was away—just to visit. 'When they were all younger, Luke and Mark and Bob, they'd all go out riding together, with her. She used to call them the Three Musketeers!' She nodded happily, lost in reminiscence. 'Aye, it'll be a posh wedding when the day comes.'

'I'm sure it will,' said Janna quietly. She felt wretched, as though she were spying, and in a sense she was. She had been prepared to hate Annabel, simply because she was loved by Luke, but it was clear that the old lady was extremely fond of her, and as Matty seemed a shrewd judge, and was nobody's fool, it was equally obvious that Annabel had everything going for her.

There was a noise outside, a clatter of hooves, and Matty's head jerked round. 'Why, speak of the devil! Looks like she's——' She got no further. The door to the garden opened, after a brief tap, and a head popped in, a voice said: 'Matty love, can I come in?' and Janna looked up, wondering if she would faint. This was the moment she had been dreading ever since she had picked up the fateful letter.

She saw a golden head, then the door opened fully, and there was Annabel. She stood just inside the doorway—and she was beautiful. There was a faintly puzzled look on her face, the merest questioning glance, then she came forward, almost shyly it seemed, and said: 'Sorry, I didn't know you'd got visitors.' She gave Janna a warm apologetic smile.

This was the ultimate test. This was like nothing that had happened before. Janna heard, as if from a distance, Matty's voice telling Annabel who she was, and that Luke was in the drawing-room with his mother, and Janna and Annabel shook hands, and Annabel said:

'I'll go and see them, if you'll excuse me?' Her handshake was warm and firm. She was roughly the same height and build as Janna, but her hair was golden, and tumbling around her face in soft waves. The tight white jodhpurs and red sweater that she wore were extremely chic. She had classical features, a laughing mouth, and deep blue eyes.

'I'll see you later,' she said softly, and went out. There was silence for a few moments, then Matty said:

'Well now, you've met her. Funny we should be talking about her.'

'Yes, wasn't it?' Janna tried to keep a calm expression on her face, but it wasn't easy. She ached inside, a dull deep ache. Luke loved that woman—and she could see why. She was lovable, and she was all woman, that was obvious, warm, friendly, nice. But would she be as nice when Luke told her how he had found Janna and brought her back? Matty had merely introduced them, not said anything else. Annabel could easily be thinking that Janna was visiting Matty.

Matty began to talk again, but Janna was only half listening. The sooner she found relatives—the sooner she left here, the better for all, particularly for herself. The sooner their brief marriage was annulled—She bit her lip. Matty, in full flow about some party years ago, wasn't aware of Janna's disquiet. She was lost in the gentle flow of reminiscence, chuckling occasionally, and Janna nodded, and made the right comments at the right moment, but inside she was numb and hurting.

Luke came in, alone. He looked at them, smiled, and said, 'Matty's giving you our family history, is she?' He went over and put his hand on the old lady's shoulder. 'I've come out to make coffee.

Don't get up, I'd hate to spoil your gossip. Just tell me where it is.'

He looked briefly at Janna. His face was serious, not smiling. She wondered what he was thinking. 'Annabel is lovely,' she said.

'She is, isn't she?' But he didn't smile as he said it. He wasn't smiling at Janna any more. He had the woman he loved with him, and he would want to get back to her.

Janna stood up. 'Let me make the coffee,' she said. 'Go back in there, I'll bring it in, or Matty will.'

'It's all right,' he said casually, and seated himself. 'She and my mother are gossiping about some dance next week.' He groaned. 'To which I will no doubt be dragged.'

Matty was looking in a cupboard and turned sharply. 'You should mix more,' she said sternly. 'Do you good to go.'

'Yes, Matty, sorry, Matty, I'll be a good boy.' The old woman snorted and began to spoon coffee into a percolator. She had her back to them, and Luke's eyes met Janna's.

'How do *you* feel about going to a dance?' he asked.

She shook her head. 'I've never been to one. I'm not sure if I can dance, anyway. I'll stay here with Matty—if she'll have me.'

'Do *you* good to go,' said Matty. 'Pretty girl like you—you'd enjoy yourself.'

I wouldn't, thought Janna, and I'd rather not. How could I enjoy myself when I saw them slip away from the crowd? She shook her head.

'You've been to a party,' Luke persisted. 'You enjoyed that.'

'At Eva's?' Did he have to remind her of their

wedding night party? For that was what it had been. 'Yes, it was—lovely——' She met his eyes, anguished.

'Well then, the dance won't be much different. It's being given by some friends of ours a few miles away.' She wanted to scream at him, to tell him to leave her alone. Couldn't he see? Was he so blind as to persist when every word he said was like a knife turning in a wound? She felt ill, suddenly, and sat down again at the table, trying to control the shaking anguish that filled her.

'What's up, love?' Matty noticed first. She looked from Janna to Luke. 'She looks tired out, poor little lass.'

'I am, rather.' Janna nodded. 'I'm sorry——'

The percolator began to bubble busily. Luke said, 'Do you want to go and lie down for a while?'

'I don't want to be a nuisance——'

'Nonsense!' Matty glanced at Luke. 'Watch that coffee, I'll take her up. Come on, my dear.'

Janna followed her out. As they crossed the hall, she could hear women's voices from the lounge, only a murmur, not the words. She went up the curving wide staircase, and along a wide carpeted corridor, and Matty opened a door at the end, into a large and beautiful bedroom, all in cream, save for the rich deep red velvet curtains. She turned down the cream furry bedspread and looked kindly at Janna. 'Take your shoes and dress off, and in you get. A lie-down will put you right, you'll see. The bathroom's next door. I'll leave the door open so's you'll see it. Now have a little sleep. I'll pop up later to look in on you.'

Janna sat down and eased off her sandals. 'Thank you, Matty,' she said. 'You're very kind.'

'Aye, well, you've been through quite a lot. No

wonder you're feeling a bit off. Just you make yourself comfy, there's a good girl.' Matty went out and closed the door. Janna took off her dress and lay down, pulling the covers up. She was exhausted. Within minutes she was fast asleep.

She didn't know how long she had slept, and when she woke up to hear the tapping on the door, she didn't for a moment remember where she was. She had been dreaming of Luke, a sad dream in which he had walked away from her towards the smiling woman who waited in a long white dress——

'Come in,' she called, and Luke entered.

'Are you feeling better?' he asked.

'Yes, much, thanks. What time is it?'

'Nearly seven.'

'Good grief! I'm sorry——' She sat up.

'It's all right,' he said soothingly, and sat at the end of the bed. 'You've not upset anyone. My mother's happy to see her wandering boy home again, and we've been talking all afternoon—and Matty's been dozing in the kitchen.'

'Where's Annabel?' What would she think about him coming up for her?

'She left an hour or so ago. My brother Mark phoned. He's driving up tonight for an hour.'

'Are you going to the dance?'

'Yes,' Luke grimaced. 'We'll persuade Mark as well. The four of us can go. You'll enjoy it.'

'If you think *I* will, why do you pull faces because *you're* going?'

He laughed. 'Clever girl! I'm not a party person, that's why. But for you—You'll meet people of your own age. You'll have fun.'

'I don't want fun—I don't want to meet people my own age,' said Janna.

'You'll feel different in a day or so. Annabel will lend you a dress—she's about your build, and she's got a wardrobe that's like Harrods' dress department.'

'Did—did you tell her how we'd met?'

'My mother did.'

'Didn't she—mind?' It was difficult to say. Why should she? Janna could be no threat to her. She must know that, she must be secure in her love for Luke, and him for her. But that she had to ask.

He smiled. Thoughtfully, he said: 'If she did, she hid it well. But she's like that.' He prodded Janna's feet under the cover. 'She's a warm, gentle person.'

'How soon are you going to be married?' she asked. She wished she hadn't the moment the words came out. He stood up.

'I don't know.' His voice had gone quiet. He walked over to the window and stood with his back to her, jingling some coins in his pocket. 'There are—certain things to be done first, as you and I know.'

'I'm sorry,' she said, wretched. 'I shouldn't have asked.' She put her head in her hands. 'We should never have——'

'Got married?' he said quietly.

'Yes.' It was a mere whisper.

Luke took a deep breath. 'You'd have been there for months more.'

'So? I could have stayed in Rio d'Oro, got a job——'

'As what?'

'I don't know.' She shook her head. 'I'd have found something—your factory perhaps.'

'Is that what you'd have preferred? To stay there?'

'It would have been better for you,' she answered

quietly. 'You've got yourself into a mess, and it's my fault. I'm so sorry. Annabel is so very nice—I liked her very much——'

Luke turned abruptly. 'For God's sake, shut up,' he said harshly, and Janna flinched with the abruptness of his words. They were as though he had struck her. She felt herself go white with the shock, and looked at him, as dazed as though he had in fact hit her. He didn't want her to talk about the woman he loved. That hurt. It was as though she weren't good enough to do so.

'I won't do it again,' she said quietly. He turned and walked out without another word, closing the door behind him.

That was it. She knew now how she had to behave. Luke had put her in her place, and she wouldn't forget it. She didn't belong here, and she wouldn't stay long, she knew that as well.

CHAPTER NINE

THE next few days passed quickly. On Monday, Luke had driven to London alone to begin his search for Janna's father's background, taking with him the written details of all she could remember, of dates, and her father's age, and his full Christian names. He had refused to take Janna, saying he worked better alone, and with this she had to be content.

Mark had arrived on the Sunday evening, totally different in personality from Luke, while bearing a resemblance to him physically. He had been charm-

ing to Janna, almost making up for Luke's quiet-
ness—which had begun after the painful brief scene
in her bedroom—and had offered his help in trying
to trace any family for her, an offer which she sensed
was sincerely meant.

Luke's mother was kind, a fact which emerged
gradually, for Janna sensed her natural reserve. But
it was as though, after Janna's story on Sunday, she
had changed. She took Janna out with her to visit
friends on the Wednesday, and they spent a pleasant
afternoon, returning in time for dinner that evening.

Of Luke she had seen hardly anything. When
they reached the house on Wednesday early evening, his car, a maroon Jaguar, was parked at the
front. Clare Hayes-Ross smiled at Janna. 'He's
back,' she said, sounding faintly surprised. He had
gone out that morning early, without saying where
he was going, and said he might be late. His mother
never asked him, she had told Janna. He had several
business interests, and he occasionally played golf
with colleagues, and took people to lunch. He had
his own private telephone in his study, and spent a
lot of time there, phoning people all over the world.
Janna had gradually realised, in the few days she
had been there, what an active man he was. Since
Sunday they had never been alone together at all.
That it was deliberate on his part Janna had no
doubt. But it was certainly so subtly done that no
one else could possibly be aware of it. Luke's
manner to her at all times was casual, polite,
friendly. Yet he had become a stranger. It was
almost impossible for her to reconcile the warm,
loving, passionate man with whom she had spent so
many hours in secret with this remote, aloof Luke
who was every inch the business man. There was a

wall between them, an invisible one, but it was there, and it was more real to Janna than anyone else.

She ached for the time when she could leave. Then she might be able to forget him. It was possible; anything was possible. Her love for him was unchanging and unfaltering, and she wanted him to be happy above all else. But he was obviously not, with her there.

The two women went into the hall, and Nero bounded up to meet them. Janna took him for long walks in the countryside around the house, and he welcomed her as enthusiastically as he did Luke and Clare.

'Down, boy, that's a good dog,' she said now. Luke emerged from his study. 'There you are,' smiled his mother. 'Are you in for dinner?'

'I am.' He smiled at them both. The smile was for his mother, Janna knew that. 'And I've told Matty—before you ask.' He patted the dog, who had transferred his affections to his master. 'Mark should be here any time too.'

'Oh, good,' said his mother, and smiled warmly at Janna. 'That's nice. It's not often I have my sons home for dinner, Janna. They're both busy men.' She sighed. 'I'll go and make myself presentable.' She already looked very smart to Janna, but then she always did.

She walked towards the stairs. It would mean Janna would be alone with him, and he wouldn't want that. 'I'll go and help Matty,' she said, and walked quickly away, without looking at Luke.

In the kitchen, Matty was singing softly to herself, as she diced carrots on the working top. A bowl of potatoes waited to be peeled, and green beans to be sliced. Janna put on an apron that lay across a chair. 'I'm here,' she said. 'Point me to the work.'

'Bless you, love. You can do the rest of the veg. Did you have a nice time?'

'Yes, thanks.' Janna began to peel busily. 'Mark's coming, isn't he? That'll be five for dinner. Are there enough potatoes here?'

'Hmm, you've got a point. Mark's got an appetite like a horse—pop in a couple more, will you—mind, on the other hand, Luke's not been eating as much——'

Janna had noticed. He ate little or nothing at breakfast each morning—but it was not for her to comment on it. The telephone now shrilled as she was about to make a noncommittal answer, and Matty said, 'Be a dear and answer it, will you? I don't suppose Luke will. He's buried in some paper-work in his room.'

Janna picked up the wall telephone by the door. It linked with five other extensions throughout the house. 'Hello,' she said.

Annabel's voice was instantly recognisable. 'Hello—Janna? It's Annabel here. Is Luke in?'

'Yes. Will you hold on a moment? I'll get him.'

'Look, not if he's busy—please don't. Would you just give him a message from me?'

'Of course I will.'

'Tell him I won't be able to see him this evening. Something's cropped up. I'll explain when I see him tomorrow. And Janna, before you go—you are going to the dance on Friday, aren't you?'

'Er—well, no, I wasn't,' Janna answered.

'Oh, but you must! You'll love it. I thought it was arranged.'

Janna bit her lip. 'It's very kind of you, but I

won't know anyone——'

'You'll know us!' Annabel laughed. 'Please come. I promise I'll look after you—and Janna, I've got some super dresses that will fit you perfectly.'

Janna felt wretched. She had only met Annabel twice: the brief time on the Sunday, and again when she had called the previous day for coffee, during which time she had been warm and friendly—genuinely so, and offered to teach Janna to ride a horse. Janna had realised then why Luke had been so curt with her on the Sunday. It was very difficult to accept such unstinted friendship without feeling wretched pangs of guilt at the terrible deception.

'Annabel, it's truly kind of you,' she said, 'but——'

'No buts. I'll call over for you in the morning and bring you back home. When you've tried on a few dresses, you'll be persuaded. See you about ten. 'Bye, Janna.'

'Goodbye—thank you.' Janna hung up.

'I'll just go and tell Luke,' she said, 'then I'll do those vegetables.'

She ran out, across to Luke's study, and knocked. 'Come in,' he called, voice abrupt.

'Annabel phoned,' said Janna. She didn't go in, merely opened the door slightly and popped her head in.

Luke stood up and walked towards her. 'Don't stand in the doorway,' he said. 'Come in.' He closed the door behind her. 'Well? What did she say?'

'She's sorry she can't see you tonight. Something's cropped up, and she'll explain when she sees you tomorrow.' She recited it parrot fashion, almost word for word, and stood away from him, ready to go the minute she had finished.

'Is that all?'

'Yes.' She leaned sideways to put her hand on the handle, but he said: 'Wait.'

She looked at him. 'I'm helping Matty with the veget——'

'Damn the vegetables!' he snapped irritably. 'They can wait a minute.'

'Of course.' She stood there very quiet, very still. It seemed important not to do anything that would irritate him further. She was a burden, she knew that now, but it was not her choice to be so. If she could leave tomorrow, she would. While she was here, though, she would be as unobtrusive as possible, and as helpful to both Matty and his mother—and to him, if he wanted her to be. Only he didn't want her in any way. She knew that.

'I've been to London again today,' he said. 'The B.M.A.—that's the British Medical Association—is doing its best, looking through various registers, but they need more information. Is there *anything* at all you can think of that you might not have told me?'

'I can't think at the moment,' she answered. That was true. Luke had a paralysing effect on her thought processes. His hostility was almost tangible. She racked her brains, and found inspiration. 'I'll have another look in that box of papers,' she said, and he snapped:

'Papers? What papers?'

'The—there are a lot of old odds and ends, and trinkets in a box I brought with me—b-but I wouldn't——'

'Good God! Why didn't you tell me before? Where is it?'

'In my case. I thought I had——'

'Dammit, I can't remember everything,' he snapped, cutting her off in mid-sentence. He raked his fingers through his hair. 'Go and get it—no, wait. Leave it until after dinner. We'll bring it in here and we'll go through it together.'

'But your brother's coming.'

'So?' He looked at her, face hard, then gave a laugh. 'Oh, I *see*——'

'What?' She looked back at him, bewildered.

'Fancy him, do you?' he grated, voice harsh, eyes dark.

'No! What a ridiculous——'

'Is it?' He took a step nearer to her. 'Come off it, Janna. You were lapping it up on Sunday.'

'Don't be stupid!' she snapped, temper flaring at the unjust and cruel taunt. She forgot all her decisions to be as inoffensive as possible. This was hateful.

'Stupid? Well, why should he be coming here twice in four days?'

'I don't know. He's *your* brother, you ask him——' She turned angrily to find the door handle and Luke caught her and whisked her round.

'Don't walk out on *me*!' he grated.

'I'm not stopping here to listen to your ridiculous——'

'You bloody well are.' He turned the key in the lock, took it out and put it in his pocket. 'You're a fast little worker, aren't you? It all adds up now. He was very keen to go to that dance the minute he thought *you'd* be there——'

She hit him hard across his face, and he went white with anger and shock. 'You little bitch!' he snapped furiously, and grabbed hold of her tightly, his fingers digging into her arms.

'Let me go,' she whispered, suddenly frightened. 'Please—let me go. I'm sorry I hit you.' Wide-eyed, she stared at him, and he released her as though he couldn't bear the touch of her.

'I don't fancy him,' she said. 'Truly.' How could she, loving Luke as she did? Only she couldn't tell him that. 'And I'm sorry if you think he likes me. I'll try to make him not—like me——' Luke didn't want her to be further involved with his family. That was understandable. But she wished she weren't so dependent on him. 'I know you don't want me here,' she went on. It was time for the truth, for plain speaking. 'And I understand why—believe me, I do understand—but please also see that I'm pretty helpless just at the moment. I can't leave—I have nowhere to go. But I—don't want to stay here longer than necessary, I promise you.' Her voice was a husky whisper. 'I know you probably regret all your generous gestures, and I'm sorry—but I swear to you now, if this is what's worrying you, that I will never give a clue to Annabel about—anything at all. I swear it.' She had finished. She could say no more to make him see. If he didn't understand now, he never would.

There was silence. It grew, and became taut, as taut as the tension which now filled the room. And somehow, Janna sensed, her words had got through to Luke. She was trembling slightly, and leaned against the door for support. He walked away from her, over to the window, and stood there looking out, and it was like a repetition of Sunday, as though it was all going to happen again, and he was going to tell her to shut up—She caught her breath. Her heart hammered violently. She went over to the window and touched his arm briefly.

'Let me go,' she said. 'I'll try and keep out of your way as much as possible, Luke, while I'm here. But Annabel's coming over for me in the morning, to take me back to her house.'

He turned at that, looking down at her, face like stone. 'Why?'

'To try on dresses. I'll phone her and tell her I can't——'

'No, don't do that. Go, in the morning, and try on the dresses.'

'But—the d-dance,' she stammered. 'You don't want—now——'

'Perhaps I was wrong,' he said harshly. 'I don't know anything any more.' He looked pale, almost ill. 'Go back and help Matty.'

'The door's locked.'

He swore softly and strode over to unlock it. Janna followed, and stumbled over a rug, and fell to her knees. Luke came over and pulled her to her feet. 'Are you all right?' he asked.

'Yes. The rug.' She looked down at it, then up at him. He held her by her arms, and she thought she saw a terrible pain in his eyes, and she said softly, 'Luke, don't you know I wouldn't do anything to hurt you?'

He closed his eyes. She couldn't see the pain there now, but she could feel it in his hands, feel the fine tremor of them as he fought for control, and she wanted to comfort him, to love him. 'Oh, Luke,' she whispered, 'please don't be hurt!'

'Dear God,' he muttered. 'It's too late for that——' and he held her to him, close, closer, until she was crushed helplessly against his chest, and she felt the trembling of his body, and wondered if he wanted to hurt her, as he was being hurt. She moaned faintly, her body helpless against the power of him. He could kill her, she knew that. He was so very strong, and he didn't even know his own strength. She felt herself going dizzy, felt herself going faint, and tried to say something, to tell him—then his lips came down on hers, his mouth harsh and brutal and savage. It was a kiss of despair, a kiss that echoed his deep dark pain. Janna was breathless, frightened, sensing the passion and anguish that went into it, but struggling, fighting for her sanity. Luke lifted his head, and she could breathe again, and she put up her shaking hands to rest at each side of his head, to steady him, to give him the strength she could hardly spare herself.

'I'll go,' she whispered, more shaken than she had ever been in her life. 'I'll leave here tomorrow.'

'Where would you go?' His voice was as ragged as if he too, found breathing difficult.

'I don't know—anywhere——' She was crying now, tears falling. 'Don't you see, it's all gone wrong—I'm no good here, and it makes you un-happy——'

'You can't leave.' It was a flat statement. 'Not now—not yet.'

'There must be hostels in London. I'd get work of some sort—I'd give you my address so that you could let me know if you find anyone—or I'd take over the search myself. There's no need for you—you have so many other jobs to do——' She steadied her voice, regaining a measure of control. Still she held him, and he had made no move to free himself. It was as if he was hardly aware that she held him. 'And you've done so much, so very much more than anyone has a right to expect. I want you to be happy, Luke, to—marry Annabel as soon as our—arrangement is annulled, and when I'm gone, you'll soon forget.'

'You cannot leave, and that's final. When I've traced your relatives. Then——' he stopped. 'Then——'

Janna took a deep breath. 'I pray it will be soon,' she whispered. 'Very soon.'

She stroked his hair, scarcely aware that she was doing so. 'I'd better go now. I'll get the box after dinner.' She took her hands away slowly. Luke didn't move. She walked away, opened the door, and went out very quietly.

Dinner was, for Janna, a very difficult meal. Mark, sitting opposite her at the dining table, seemed pre-occupied, Luke scarcely spoke at all, and it was left to the three women to make the conversation. Clare Hayes-Ross, if she was aware of any constraint in the air, ignored it completely. Mark caught Janna's eye at one point and gave a slight smile. He was nice, and she liked him, but after Luke's startling accusations she felt very ill at ease whenever he so much as glanced at her.

It was a relief to be able to escape with Matty to fetch in the sweet, a delicious concoction of straw-berries and meringue, and when at last that had been eaten, and they got up to go to the drawing-room for coffee, Luke said to Janna: 'Go and get your box, Janna. We'll have our coffee in my study.'

'Really, Luke,' his mother protested, 'can't it wait a while? Mark's here——'

'But not for long, Mother,' Mark answered. 'I have to dash. I'm seeing a fellow near here tonight later, and I couldn't resist one of Matty's delicious meals.'

Clare sighed. 'Good grief, you've only just ar-rived. You men!' She looked at Janna and shook her head. 'Don't have sons, my dear, they treat their homes like hotels!'

Mark kissed his mother's cheek. 'You cut me to the quick, darling,' he said lightly. 'Tell you what—

I'll come over on Friday and spend all afternoon with you. How's that?'

She looked at him suspiciously, amusement not far away. 'Hmmm, let me guess why—what do you want?'

'Nothing! Just to see you.'

They wandered out, and Luke and Janna were left alone. She began to stack the plates and he helped her. She hoped he wasn't going to comment on Mark's plans to come on Friday, and said quickly: 'I'll take these out and get my box. I'll bring your coffee in to your study if you want to go there now.' She picked up the plates, moved a spoon slightly that was in danger of falling, and went out. Luke hadn't said a word.

Janna found the box and ran down with it to the kitchen, where Matty was just about to pour out the coffee. 'Can I wash up later?' she asked the old woman. 'Only Luke and I are going to look through some papers——'

'Off you go. I'll do these, it's no trouble.'

'If you're sure——' Janna said doubtfully.

'I'm sure. Take your coffee.'

'Thanks, Matty.' She tucked the box under her arm, picked up the cups and saucers, and went out. Luke's study door was open, and she went in. He stood by his desk. He had cleared a space of papers, and took the coffee from her to put down there.

Janna placed the box in the large space. 'Is it locked?' he asked.

'No.' She opened it, and it was crammed with papers which spilled out. She began to remove them, lifting them out carefully. He pulled up two chairs, side by side, and asked:

'Can I start going through these?'

'You can search through everything. I've nothing

to hide,' she said. The box brought back a rush of memories, and they were painful, one reason she had, in a way, scarcely thought of it recently. It was precious to her, but more in the way that some valuable old ornament would be, something that was there; to be looked at, but not touched too often.

Luke read quickly, eyes skimming the faded papers, bills, old letters from so many years ago that Janna had never been sure who some of the people were. Yet her father had treasured the box, and therefore she did as well. Luke placed them carefully into two piles when finished, one much bigger than the other, and all the papers were out now. Janna saw the various small trinkets in the base of the box—a small doll, made of wood, no longer than a match, yet exquisitely carved, and dressed, an ivory elephant no bigger than her thumbnail, a small gold ring with an amethyst, a gold locket on a chain . . . souvenirs of childhood that now seemed part of another world, another time.

Luke had sorted the papers meticulously into two piles, and put the larger one back in the box, after removing the locket and ring. 'There's nothing in that lot,' he said. 'I don't need them. But these——' he tapped the smaller pile, 'I'm going to go through again.' He picked up the locket and turned it over in his hands. 'Does this open?'

'No.'

'Are you sure?' He picked up a small magnifying glass and examined the locket carefully. 'Janna, look in that top right-hand drawer. There's a small box—get it.'

She did so, found the small leather box, and handed it to him. He put down the locket and glass, opened the box, and extracted a fine needle-like instrument.

'What are you doing?' she queried.

'Going to open this,' he answered.

'But it doesn't——'

He looked up. 'Doesn't it? We'll see.' He bent to his task, and she watched him, disbelieving but fascinated. He probed as delicately as any jeweller at the side of the locket, his face deeply concentrating on his task. His hands were large, tanned, the backs covered with fine dark hair, but his fingers were careful and gentle. How well she knew that. . . .

'Ah!' He looked up. The locket lay open in his hand. Inside were two very small photos.

He held up the locket so that Janna could see, and silently handed her the magnifying glass. She took it and focussed it on the two images. 'That one is my father when he was younger,' she said. 'The other one must be——' she struggled to speak, 'Mother.' It was like looking at a picture of herself.

'May I take them out?' he asked gently.

She nodded, and he probed again, with infinite care, and removed the tiny photographs. There was writing on the back of both, faded and indistinct, but Luke looked carefully, then began to write on a notepad. When he had finished, he looked up. His face was serious. 'You'd better sit down.'

She did so. He tapped the stack of papers, still on the desk. 'I think I can tie up several things,' he said. 'Now—first, Janna, your name's not Thorne. It's Stewart.' She sat there very still, her hands clasped tightly together on her lap. 'Your parents were married in 1955. The date's here—October the second—and with the information we'll be able to check up far more than we would before.' He looked steadily at her. 'Look carefully at both photos. I think they are your parents' wedding pictures—or one of them, that were cut up and put in the locket.

Is that your father's writing?'

She examined it carefully. 'No. So it must have been my mother's.'

'Yes, undoubtedly. I think you must be prepared for the fact that some time between 1955 and 1960 something happened to make him not only leave Britain with your mother to go and live in South America, but to change his name—therefore yours.'

She swallowed. 'I'd already guessed that,' she whispered. 'But it doesn't make any difference. I still want to—to find——'

'Of course you do.' Luke stood up. 'And that's what we're going to do.' He looked at the clock. 'We'd better go and join my mother and Mark.' His eyes met hers briefly as he said his brother's name, and Janna met his look without expression. She had enough to think about at that moment without being concerned in his opinion of her as a brother-snatcher.

'I'd rather go and see if Matty needs any help, if you don't mind,' she said quietly. 'Shall I leave the box here?'

'Yes. I'll put everything back when I've copied what I need.'

The interview, the brief cessation of hostilities, was over. She stood up and went to the door, looked back once at Luke, and went out. She felt at home with Matty. She trusted the old woman, and liked her very much.

Luke's mother was a pleasant and controlled woman, yet Janna had occasionally found Clare Hayes-Ross looking at her as if puzzled—as if she was made uneasy by this stranger from a foreign land. She was never anything else but charming—but Janna, with her own sure feminine instinct, realised why the other woman had her reservations. She was clearly fond of Annabel, and therefore wanted her as a daughter-in-law.

She had said as much one day, when she and Janna had been drinking coffee in the drawing-room, told her that she had never had a daughter, but that Annabel would have been the ideal one if she could have had.

Her smile had been warm as she said it, and then she had gone on to say how fond she was of Annabel's parents, and later, during the same conversation, she had asked Janna how old she was.

'Nearly twenty?' she had said, after Janna had told her. 'How young—and how lucky, to have all your life stretching ahead of you.' She had smiled gently. 'I was engaged at nineteen—thought I'd never been so happy in my life, and was in fact within only a few weeks of my wedding when I met Luke's father, my late husband—and that was that! The engagement was discreetly broken off, and six months later we were married.' She laughed. 'Make the most of the next year or so—you'll fall in love several times, my dear. This is the time for finding out.'

Janna had smiled in return, nodded, agreed—but inside, she knew the truth. The one truth she could never speak. She loved Luke, and always would. It had been Clare Hayes-Ross's gentle way of warning her not to fall for Luke. She couldn't know it was already too late.

She put a bright smile on her face and went into the kitchen.

Janna prepared herself for Annabel's arrival the following morning with some trepidation. She rose

early, had a bath and washed her hair, which was
growing very satisfactorily, and with its natural
wave, was now fashionably elfin-looking. A little
lipstick, carefully applied—she was still not used to
it—and she was ready, in yellow sun-dress and sandals. Matty was in the kitchen preparing breakfast,
and Janna helped her, only too relieved to take her
mind off the visit to Annabel's house. She felt as
though she were a traitor to the other girl. Annabel's kindness was only added salt in the wound.
She understood full well how Luke felt, and why he
was bad-tempered with her. He didn't need a re-
minder of his infidelity—it was obviously tearing at
him in so many ways already.

Promptly at ten, Annabel drove up in a smart
blue sports car, had a brief chat with Luke's mother,
who was busy addressing invitation cards for a charity function she was shortly to hold at Courthill,
then went to find Janna in the kitchen. She wore a
silky dress, very slim-fitting, in a delicate shade of
rose, and her long legs were very tanned.

'Hello.' She greeted both Matty and Janna
warmly, and sat down. 'Any chance of a cup of
coffee before we go, Matty?'

'Course you can, my dear.' Matty was only too
happy to be looking after someone. The whine of
the Hoovers came from another part of the house, as
the cleaners and housekeeper busied themselves
keeping it immaculate. The place was run like a
smoothly oiled machine.

Annabel grinned at Janna. 'My mother's looking
forward to meeting you,' she told her, and stretched
herself, like a luxurious cat. 'She'd like you to stay
for lunch—with Matty's permission, of course.' This
with a mischievous look in Matty's direction,

who snorted derisively.

'You'd think I was an old terror or something,' she grumbled, but complacently.

'You are, Matty, you are! We're all scared of you.'

'Hmm, looks like it, when you come asking me for cups of coffee!'

'Well, will you? Would you like to? Luke's mother won't mind. She's doing her charity bit all day, visiting the old dears at the home near the village.'

'I'd like to. Thank you,' Janna answered. There was no reasonable way she could refuse. Luke had left immediately after breakfast, for London, he had said.

They all sat down to drink coffee, and a plate of Matty's home-made biscuits was produced, while Annabel chatted to the old lady, passing on various titbits of gossip about people Janna had never heard of, but found interesting. Her talk wasn't malicious, but amusing, and Matty was clearly enjoying herself.

Then Annabel looked at her watch. 'Better go,' she said. 'Ready, Janna?'

'Yes, I'll get my bag.'

'Thank you for the coffee, Matty. I'll be back for another cup later—if you'll have me.' To Janna, as she went out, she said: 'I'll be in the car at the front.'

Five minutes later they were on their way. Annabel drove fast down the narrow country lane that passed the house, and said, above the noise of the engine: 'I don't live far—we'll be there in a couple of minutes. Do you drive, Janna?'

'Not legally. I have done sometimes—but the roads near my home were very different from these in England.'

'I'm sure. You must find everything here very new and strange.'

'Yes, I do. We lived very simply, Dad and I. I'd never even seen a television till I was in the hotel——' Janna stopped, horror flooding her in a wave as she realised what she had said. Annabel had the impression that Luke and Janna had arrived in England on Sunday morning. Quickly she went on: 'The traffic too—it's frightening. I keep thinking we're on the wrong side of the road.'

Annabel laughed. The moment had passed, and there was no comment. She hadn't noticed anything. 'Here we are,' she said, and swung into a driveway. There were other houses that they had passed, spaced far away, from each other, as had been Eva's and Luis's home in Rio d'Oro, and indeed there was the same atmosphere of luxury in the area.

The house was a large white one, in green and pleasant gardens, well tended, and with many trees. Annabel stopped by the wide pillared entrance, and they both got out. 'I'll take you up to my room,' she said, 'and we'll have a leisurely trying on session, then lunch with my mama. Do come in.' She led the way, up the steps into a beautiful hall, and up a wide staircase. Annabel opened a door and they were in a large bedroom, extremely feminine, with lacy net curtains at the windows, and a thick soft cream carpet and light elegant furniture. Annabel kicked off her sandals and turned to Janna. 'Make yourself at home,' she said. 'I'll pour us a drop of wine—very naughty, but why not?' She smiled. 'Then I've got something rather personal to ask you.' Janna looked at her, and her heart started to thud. She had a sudden, dreadful premonition.

CHAPTER TEN

ANNABEL went over to her dressing-table. On it was a bottle of wine and two glasses. Back to Janna she asked: 'Do you smoke?'

'No.' Janna waited.

'Mind if I do?' She turned and handed Janna a glass. 'Cheers.'

'Cheers. No, of course not.'

Annabel opened a cigarette box and took one out. She lit it and blew out smoke. 'That's better. Do sit down, Janna.'

Janna sat on a chair by the window, holding her glass. She looked up at Annabel and saw that her face had gone serious, no more smiles now. 'You said you had something rather personal to ask me,' Janna said, and took one sip of the cool white wine.

Annabel bit her lip. For the first time she looked unsure of herself, her beautiful face rather paler than usual. 'Are you in love with Luke, Janna?' she asked.

Although it was the question that Janna had instinctively feared, it still hit her with the force of a blow, and she went dizzy with shock, and for a moment could scarcely breathe. Anguished, she looked up at the girl who waited there, then took a deep breath. She could not lie—yet she could not hurt her. She had no wish to do that, ever. 'I like him very much,' she whispered. 'He's been so kind——'

'But *do* you love him?' Annabel persisted.

Janna's mouth trembled. The glass in her hand shook. 'Yes,' she whispered. 'I'm sorry—I can't lie to you——'

'Does he love you?'

She looked up at that. This was one question she could answer with complete honesty. 'No,' she said. 'Oh *no*—he loves you, Annabel, very much—and I know why he does. He has no idea I love him, I promise you that, and he never will.' She could even manage a smile. 'He wants me to leave—I think he regrets asking me to stay now, but he's trying to trace my relatives, you see, and I've nowhere to go, but I swear to you that I'll leave his house as soon as possible.' She touched the rim of her glass, stroking it until it made a faint humming sound. 'I'm sorry if I've upset you by being there——' she faltered. How could this sophisticated, assured, beautiful woman be worried by Janna? Perhaps her love for Luke was so great that she feared—was vulnerable. Janna wanted only to reassure her. 'But you have nothing to fear from me. He—he doesn't even—like me——' She stopped, her precarious self-control faltering.

'Oh, Janna, I'm sorry! Don't upset yourself, please.' Annabel came over to where she sat and rested her hand on Janna's shoulder. 'Please don't cry, or you'll have me crying too. I can understand you loving Luke. He's rather a wonderful man——' She moved away. 'Please try and forget I asked.'

That was asking the impossible. 'Is that why you brought me here?' asked Janna. 'Because you had to know?'

'Only partly. We came here so that you could borrow a dress for the dance, remember?'

Janna looked up at her. 'It might be better if I didn't go,' she said unhappily.

'No.' Annabel shook her head. 'No, if you don't go, then neither shall I.' She sat down on the bed. 'It's all right, Janna. I know it hurts to love someone when they don't love you—it hurts like hell—but you can't run away and hide. You have to put on a brave face.'

Janna smiled. How easy to talk, when you were as sure of someone's love as Annabel must be. 'You're right, of course,' she said quietly.

'Well then, let's find something rather super for you, shall we?' Annabel flung out her arm towards the long wardrobe lining one wall of the room. 'Just so long as you don't set your heart on the dress I've bought for myself!'

'I wouldn't do that.' Janna put her glass down on the glass top that covered and protected the delicate wood of the dressing-table. 'You're a wonderful person, Annabel,' she said. 'In your place I'm not sure if I could find it in my heart to actually be kind to someone who'd just told me she loved my fiancé.' She swallowed. 'I'm glad Luke loves you—I'd hate him to—to marry someone not as nice——' She bit her lip, and Annabel turned away suddenly and went to the window with her back to Janna. She stood there rubbing her arms, as if she was cold.

'Oh, God!' The words said by Annabel were so quiet that Janna scarcely heard, and she knew they had not been said to her, or perhaps even for her to hear.

Then, the next moment, Annabel turned round again, and she was blinking away tears. She gave a shaky laugh. 'There, you've got me at it!' she said. 'Aren't we a pair of idiots? Men! The trouble they cause!' She went to the wardrobe and slid the door back on its runners. 'I know we won't forget what's been said, but let's try, shall we?' She ran her hand along the rows of long dresses that hung there. 'Come and have a look.'

Janna went and stood beside her. It was said now, her secret out. Annabel was surely the last person she would ever have dreamed of telling. Janna had to live with the awareness that Annabel could tell Luke. There was nothing she could do about that, and she would not beg her not to. She took a deep breath, and touched some soft silky blue material.

'They're lovely,' she said. 'Oh, so *many!*'

'Yes, dozens. Let's get some out. We'll put them on the bed, and then begin.' The next few minutes were spent lifting out hangers and laying the fabulous collection on the bed, and Janna saw one and asked:

'May I try this one first?' It was deep blue velvet, slim-fitting at the waist and flaring to a full wide skirt. A very simple style, it had a V neck and long tightly fitting sleeves, and a row of tiny buttons down the back.

'You've got a shrewd eye for clothes,' said Annabel, and chuckled. 'I had that for my twenty-first party—and I've always loved it. Let's see how it looks on, shall we?'

She adjusted the cheval glass in the corner, pulling it out slightly so that Janna would be able to look at her reflection in a better light, while Janna slipped off her dress.

Then Annabel helped her put it on, and did up the buttons, murmuring: 'That's the only trouble with this—you need help putting it on and getting it off—damn! I've snagged my nail. Hang on a moment—*don't* look yet—I'll find my nail scissors.'

Janna obediently kept her eyes away from the mirror and waited while Annabel ruffled through a drawer. The dress was a fraction long, but so far, even without all the buttons fastened, it fitted like a dream.

'That's it. Here we go. Now, close your eyes.' She was guided over to the mirror, and Annabel said: 'Open them.'

Janna did so. Her mouth fell open. 'Oh!' she gasped.

Annabel laughed. 'It's gorgeous! Truly. You're so dark and I'm so fair—and I'll swear it suits you better than me. Turn round.' Janna turned slowly, and looked at the girl who stood watching her with a critical eye. 'Stop!' Annabel commanded. 'Wait. It's a trifle long—but it won't be with shoes on.' She looked at Janna's sandals. 'You need high ones. What shoe size are you?'

'I don't know in English sizes. Yours are different, aren't they?'

'Yes.' Annabel opened a drawer at the bottom of the wardrobe. It was filled with rows of shoes. She lifted out a pair of very high-heeled silver slippers. 'Try those.' Janna put them on, and they fitted her. 'That's it,' said Annabel. 'That is perfect.'

'Oh.' Janna looked down at her feet. She was at least three inches taller. 'I feel as if I'm going to fall over!'

'You'll have to practise. Keep them on while you try on a few more—although I think we've found the perfect dress first time.' Annabel undid the buttons, the dress was laid over the chair, and both of them sorted through and found several more dresses. All were duly tried on, all were nice—but both knew it was a formality.

Janna found, to her surprise, that she was enjoying herself. It was easy to relax with Annabel, even after that very frank and distressing conversation, because both were determined to put it behind them. And Annabel was genuinely warm and kind. Janna had wanted—had expected—to dislike her, but she liked her very much.

'It's no good, is it? We're wasting our time,' said Annabel at last, when a dozen dresses had been laid out and put back. 'We both know that the blue velvet is yours. Come one, let's put the others away. Try it again, and we'll go down and show my mother.'

Janna put it on, with the comfortable feeling of meeting an old friend again. It was fastened, checked in the mirror, then Annabel said: 'I'd like you to accept it as a gift, Janna—if you want it.'

'Oh, Annabel!' Wide-eyed, Janna turned to her. 'I couldn't!'

'Do you like it or not?'

'It's beautiful, simply beautiful,' Janna admitted, 'but——'

'Then it's yours. I won't wear it again, I know that, and it's just sitting in my wardrobe—I would very much like you to keep it.'

Janna did something on impulse that, had she thought about it, she would have hesitated to do. She turned and hugged Annabel. For a moment she sensed the other girl's brief surprise and was dismayed by her own oddness—then Annabel hugged her in return, and laughed softly.

'Oh, Janna, you're so sweet,' she said, as both drew apart. 'Truly. I'm sorry you won't be staying long—I feel we could easily become friends.' She smiled at Janna. 'There are only a few nice people about, but you're one of them—promise me, when you leave, you'll keep in touch?'

Janna nodded. 'Of course.' She turned away on the pretence of gathering up the full skirt preparatory to walking, and it hid her sudden sadness.

For of course she could not. All ties must be severed
when she left. She was as much a betrayer as was
Luke. If Annabel knew the full truth, she would be
hurt beyond words. The only chance lay in Janna
moving as far away as possible, and never seeing
Luke again—and that, naturally, would mean not
seeing Annabel. For how could she keep in touch
with one and not the other, when they were at last
married?

'I'm his wife,' she wanted to say. 'He can't marry
you until his marriage to me is annulled. And I hate
myself for what I've done, and I'm sorry, but you'll
never know how much, and it's a secret I have to
bear, for I would never hurt you by telling you. And
you said I'm nice—but you're wrong, I'm not—and
I feel terrible.'

'Let's go down. Wait, though—do you have any
jewellery?'

'No.' Janna shook her head, thinking, I've got a
simple wooden cross, and a gold wedding ring, but
they're safely hidden away in my handbag, and I
couldn't wear those.

'I'll lend you something, just to go round your
neck. I've a very simple pendant that goes beautifully with that dress. You can return it any time
after the party.' Annabel went over and opened a
leather box on her dressing-table, searched through
it and lifted out a thin gold chain on which hung an
oval bluey-mauve stone set in gold. She fastened it
on. 'There, that's perfect. Take a look.'

Janna peered in the dressing-table mirror. 'Thank
you, it's lovely. I'll take care of it. What's the
stone?'

'An amethyst—Luke bought it for me a couple of
years ago.'

Janna touched the cool stone. Luke had bought

it, and given it to Annabel with love. 'Won't he
mind?' she asked.

'No, of course not. Let's go down. Then there's
just time to change again before lunch.'

Janna followed her out, tottering a little on the
high heels. She would never get used to them,
surely, but she would do her best. She wondered
what Annabel's mother would be like.

It was Friday evening, and Janna was nearly ready.
Luke had driven over to fetch Annabel early, because she had telephoned and asked him to. She had
also asked him to tell Janna that she was bringing
something for her, and he had duly passed the message on before leaving.

Janna went up to change and was brushing her
hair when there was a tap on the door, and Annabel
came in, looking radiant in a flame-coloured dress of
swirly chiffon that emphasised her slender figure to
perfection. 'Hello,' she said. She was carrying a
small case and a silver evening bag. She put the
silver bag down on the bed.

'You look lovely,' said Janna.

'Thank you. I've brought that evening bag for
you, to go with your shoes—how are they, by the
way?'

'I totter a bit, but I'm learning fast,' Janna
answered.

'Good. I've also brought some make-up. You
don't have any, do you?'

'Some lipstick, that's all.'

'I thought so. Well, will you let me help you to
make up? You don't need much—hardly any—but
I know a few little tricks that will definitely show
you off to the best advantage.'

Slightly bewildered, Janna thanked Annabel. She

hadn't expected this. She sat down as instructed, putting a towel round her shoulders, and faced the mirror. Annabel opened the case, to reveal a very businesslike assortment of creams and powders and eyeshadows and lipsticks and blushers. Janna gazed at it in astonishment.

Annabel set to work, and subtly and quickly Janna was transformed. She wouldn't have said how or why it worked—but she definitely looked, and felt, different. It took Annabel several minutes to make up her eyes, and when she looked again the effect was startling. She peered closer, and blinked. Her eyes looked darker, lustrous, larger. 'Mmm— wow!' she said softly, and Annabel laughed.

'There—all done. I'll leave this lot here and collect it on Sunday—you look smashing, Janna.'

'Thank you. I feel—smashing.' Janna smoothed her cheek. 'I look a lot different.' She turned round to face Annabel, who was touching up her own glossy red lips. 'Why?'

'Why what?' Annabel looked at her from her own mirror.

'Why should you help me?'

'Because I haven't got a sister to share things like this with—and because I like you. Come on, let's go down and knock 'em dead!'

They gathered up their possessions and went out.

Luke and Mark were drinking whisky in the lounge and talking to their mother. Janna hadn't seen either of them changed, and caught her breath. No greater contrast could be imagined between the man who stood in the room, and who had turned slightly at her and Annabel's entrance, and the man who had walked into the bar that fateful night in Santa Cruz. This was a tall, powerful-looking man—yes, as he had been then too—but this one was clean shaven, darkly handsome, tanned, and immaculately dressed in evening suit, with black bow tie at the neck of a dazzling white shirt. He looked at Janna, and she glimpsed something like shock in his eyes before it vanished—and it might have been her imagination.

'It seems we have two beautiful women to take to the ball,' he murmured, and Mark nodded, smiled at them both.

'Indeed we do,' he agreed.

'How lovely you both look,' Clare exclaimed, and stood up to walk over to them. 'Let me see you both properly.' She regarded them both with a practised eye. 'Mmm, yes. I'd love to see Paula de Vere's face when you two walk in. Do tell me, won't you?'

Mark laughed. 'Mother dear, I never knew you were catty!'

'I'm not, darling, I'm not,' she murmured, and exchanged a glance with Annabel, who said drily:

'I'll let you know,' and laughed.

During this little exchange, which Luke hadn't joined in, Janna found her eyes drawn towards him, and as she looked, so did he turn, and then his eyes were upon her. For a moment it seemed as if there were only the two of them in the room; all else faded away, and she felt a tremor seize her. How deeply she loved him he would never know. Her eyes were dark and lustrous, and they shone with the light of her love, and she couldn't help it—then he turned away as if she had offended him.

'It's time we left,' he said. The spell was broken.

'Have a lovely evening my dears. And please try not to wake me up when you come in.'

Luke kissed his mother lightly. 'We won't,' he promised.

They all went in Mark's Daimler, the two men at

the front, Janna and Annabel at the back. Janna felt
apprehensive, and the reasons were so complex that
she couldn't even begin to analyse them, so she sat
back and tried to relax, letting the conversation flow
round her, happy to listen.

The dance was being held at a large mansion several miles away in the opposite direction from Annabel's home. When they reached the drive, it was
already lined with cars, and noise and music rocked
out to reach them as they parked the car and began
the long walk towards the front entrance. The house
was a blaze of light, spilling out down the drive,
making the trees vivid green where it touched. The
door was open wide and three guests stood talking in
the hall. Behind them, more men and women, in
small groups, drinking, laughing, enjoying themselves. The party at Eva's had prepared Janna
slightly for this kind of event. That had been her
first ever. This, the second, was different because she
was in England, and she was technically with Mark,
who took her arm as Luke and Annabel walked on
in.

'Okay?' he asked.

'Yes, fine.' She smiled gratefully at him. So like
Luke, and yet not Luke. Their voices were similar,
and their eyes, and she liked him, but she didn't
love him, and she knew that, whatever Luke
thought, Mark didn't in any way fancy her, but he
was kind and polite, and it wouldn't be his fault if
she didn't have a pleasant evening.

'You look really lovely,' he said, 'so let's sail in
and knock 'em dead.' It was the same expression
that Annabel had used, and it made her feel better.

'Right,' she smiled. 'We will!'

And so it proved. Their host and hostess—old

friends of Luke, Mark, and Annabel—welcomed Janna like an equally old friend, and she was introduced to the crowd, and given a drink, and never left alone for a moment. They all danced the evening away, and Janna had several dances with other men, and if Luke was bored he didn't show it; he was bland and charming, and it was very obvious to Janna that he and Mark were popular with nearly everybody—especially the women.

She and Annabel escaped to the cloakroom for a breather late in the evening, and Annabel asked: 'Well, how's it going?'

'I'm having a very interesting time,' Janna said truthfully. 'Although my feet are slightly killing me!'

Annabel was touching her hair with a comb, looking in the mirror, and glanced up at her, amused. 'The price we pay for beauty, my dear,' she murmured. 'Did you see that outrageously dressed woman glaring daggers at you a while ago?'

'The one in the black dress?'

'Yes. Dracula's bride. *That's* Paula de Vere.'

'I wasn't introduced to her, I don't think.'

Annabel laughed. 'No, you wouldn't be. She thinks she's the queen of society round here—I think you and I have put her nose slightly out of joint. She's been keeping well away from us for obvious reasons.'

'Is she married?'

'At the moment, no. She collects husbands. I think she's had four so far——'

'Golly!' Wide-eyed, Janna stared at her. 'She's with a very handsome man——'

'Bertie? He's a fool. I hope she doesn't make him husband number five, although I wouldn't bet on it. She used to fancy Luke. Had quite a thing about him at one time—which is why, you'll notice, he's not leaving our sides.' She chuckled. 'Nor Mark.' She stood up. 'Let's go back and rescue our men from her clutches. She'll have been watching us.'

Indeed she had. She was talking to Luke and Mark as Janna and Annabel sailed down the stairs, and looked up. Her hand was resting on Luke's arm, and he had his head bent slightly to hear her. The man who was her escort was nowhere to be seen in the crush of people milling round.

As the two girls neared the men, she turned away and was swallowed up by the crowd, and Luke turned. 'Thank God, the cavalry's arrived,' he muttered, while Mark shook with silent laughter.

'What was all that about?' queried Annabel, fixing both men with an accusing eye.

'Paula homed in the minute you'd gone,' Mark told them. 'She was making the most blatant advances to Luke. I blushed for shame.' Annabel turned to him.

'You should have rescued him,' she said.

'Not me!' He looked alarmed. 'I'm too young!'

Janna looked at Luke. He was watching his brother and Annabel talking, and he seemed not to be listening, as if the lighthearted conversation didn't concern him at all. She wondered what he was thinking. She wondered where he was, in his mind.

He cut in, in the middle of their banter. 'I'm bored,' he said.

All three stared at him. 'Good gracious,' said Annabel gently. 'It's not done to say things like that at one of Ronnie and Helen's little get-togethers! Whatever will people think?'

'I don't really care,' he answered. 'Look around —listen, it's all shallow and artificial. They're all phoneys, the bloody lot of them.'

Mark's eyes met Annabel's. Quietly she said to Luke: 'Don't you feel well?'

He looked at her and smiled faintly. 'There's nothing wrong with me, if that's what you mean.'

'But you've had enough?'

'Oh, yes, I've had enough all right. I'd had enough the minute I arrived.'

Mark looked at the silent Janna, who had said not a word in this exchange. It was not her place to do so. He lifted one eyebrow and smiled slightly apologetically. 'Do you want to leave, Luke?' he said to his brother. 'Because if you do, I'll run you home.'

'Darling, if Luke goes, we'll all go,' said Annabel.

There was a moment's silence. Janna held her breath. Something was suddenly terribly wrong, but she didn't know what it was. The air bristled with tension in their little group, which was surrounded by music and laughter, none of which seemed to touch them. For her, it didn't matter. She would be quite happy to agree to whatever was decided. It was past midnight and Annabel had told her that the parties normally went on until six or seven, the guests ending up eating breakfast before they left. She didn't think she'd manage to stay awake that long, but she wouldn't dream of saying so.

'I'm not going to spoil it for everyone else,' said Luke.

'Don't be silly, darling.' Annabel looked round. 'I'll see Ronnie and Helen, explain that we've all got to be up early——'

'Janna?' It was Luke. For the first time in an hour, he actually looked at her. 'Do you want to stay?'

'No.' She shook her head. 'I was just wondering

how I'd manage to keep awake much longer, to be truthful—but I've had a lovely time.'

'It's decided,' said Mark. 'Look, slip out to the car, you two. Annabel and I will go and find Ronnie.' He handed Luke his keys, then he and Annabel turned away and were swallowed up in the crowd.

'Come on,' said Luke, and led Janna to the still open door. Outside, couples were kissing, or dancing, or talking. It was a warm night for England, but Janna shivered.

Luke opened the driver's door and leaned in, opening the back one for Janna to get in. Then he went round to the front passenger door and slid in. She sat behind him, looked at him. He turned. 'Okay,' he said. 'Why don't you say it?'

'Say what?' She was puzzled.

'Tell me what a miserable bastard I am.'

She looked steadily at him. 'Would it make you feel better if I did?' she asked.

'No. But I can tell you're thinking it——'

'You can't tell what I'm thinking at all,' she answered steadily. 'Tell me this, though. Why do you go in the first place if you don't intend to try and enjoy yourself?'

He turned away and didn't answer. Stung by his rudeness, Janna leaned forward and snapped 'There's no need to be rude as well!'

'Annabel likes parties,' he said flatly.

'Then don't you think you might make the effort for the woman you love?'

'I did. Satisfied?'

'No.' She sat back. 'But it's obviously no use talking to you when you're in such a foul mood.' She took off the shoes and rubbed her feet. 'I'll shut up, don't worry, Luke. It's far better if I do.'

Two figures approached the car, Annabel and Mark. They slid in, and Mark turned. 'All is well,' he said. 'They won't even miss us. Let's go.' He started the motor and reversed down to the gate, while Annabel and Janna ducked their heads.

'Coming in for a drink, Annabel, or do you want me to drop you home?'

'It's on the way, I'll come in for a minute or two.' Annabel winked at Janna. 'Just one, though. Well, how did it go for you?'

'Lovely! I've taken my shoes off—they were super shoes, Annabel, but——'

'I know,' Annabel chuckled. 'Don't tell me!' She bent and took her own off. 'Ah, that's better! I'm not sorry to have left, myself, to be quite honest. It was rather noisy.'

The house was in darkness, save for a light in the hall, and when they opened the door, Nero bounded out and vanished towards the trees. They crept into the dining-room, and Luke switched on a standard lamp which gave off a soft warm glow. 'What will you have?' he asked.

'Martini for me,' said Annabel.

'And me,' added Janna.

'Mark?' Luke was busy with the glasses and bottles.

Mark looked up from the fireplace where he was poking the dying embers of a log fire. 'Oh, I'll have a coffee, I think. As it's early, I might as well get back to London tonight. I'll go and make myself one,' and so saying, he went out.

Luke handed them two glasses and poured himself a liberal measure of whisky, at which Annabel raised her eyebrows gently. 'Darling,' she said, 'if you're driving me home——'

He looked at his glass, then at her. 'I've not had much,' he said, and drank it. Janna sipped her Martini. They were going to quarrel, she sensed the brittle atmosphere very strongly. She didn't want to be there when they did.

'Excuse me——' She got up. 'I'll go and make a coffee for myself. Want one, anyone?'

Luke and Annabel were looking at each other. They might not have heard her. The atmosphere bristled. Janna slipped quietly out and went to the kitchen where the kettle boiled. Mark was just letting in the whining dog at the back door. He turned.

'Hello,' he said. 'Come to help?'

'I thought I'd have a coffee as well,' answered Janna, and sat down.

'Jolly good.' He put another beaker out. 'It's instant, I'm afraid, I can't be bothered with the percolator at this time of night.'

'That's all right.'

He grinned at her. 'Sorry about Luke,' he said. 'I don't know what got into him.' He switched off the gas, spooned coffee into the beakers, and added the water. 'Perhaps he's not well. It didn't spoil your evening, did it?'

'No, you looked after me very well. Thank you, Mark.'

'Least I could do—and besides, it's very nice to take a pretty girl to a dance, you know. There were one or two looking at me enviously!'

Janna smiled at his gallantry. He picked up the beakers. 'Come on, love, let's go and drink these in there.'

She hoped they weren't fighting. There were no sounds from the drawing-room, and the door was closed. She opened it for Mark, and for one terrible moment thought she might have interrupted them kissing—but they weren't. Annabel sat on the settee, while Luke had poured himself another glass of whisky and was drinking it. The atmosphere could have been cut with a knife. Mark glanced quickly at them both, then, as he handed Janna her beaker, gave her an odd, questioning look. There was no way she could tell him.

Annabel looked up brightly at them. 'Well,' she said, 'that's another party over. Oh, Janna, could I take the pendant tonight? Then I won't forget it.'

'Of course,' Janna put her beaker down and unfastened the clasp. 'And thank you for lending it to me.'

'A pleasure.' Annabel put it in her evening bag. 'The shoes and make-up will do any time, but I don't want to lose this.'

She had finished her drink, and stood up. 'I'd better go. I'm rather tired,' she said, with a look at Luke.

'Look, I'm going back to London,' said Mark. 'Why don't I drop you off?'

Luke deliberately took a deep swallow. Janna saw Mark's eyes on him. 'Good idea,' he said.

Annabel came over to hug Janna. 'I'll probably see you tomorrow,' she said. 'Shall I phone?'

'Yes,' Janna nodded.

Annabel went over to Luke. ''Night, darling,' she said, and kissed him, on his cheek. He held her briefly, then let her go.

Mark stood in the doorway, jingling his keys, and Janna and Luke followed them into the hallway.

They watched as the Daimler drove away, then Luke shut and bolted the door. His face was hard, almost grim. Silently, Janna walked back into the lounge, picked up shoes and bag, and said to him, 'Goodnight, Luke.'

'Goodnight.' He crossed over to the drinks cabinet. She watched him pick up the bottle.

'Don't you think——' she began.

'No, I don't,' he said curtly, and stared stonily at her. 'This is my house. If I want to get drunk I will.' He poured himself a measure, raised the glass, and said mockingly: 'Cheers.'

Janna turned and walked out without another word. She had reached her room and was about to take off the dress when she remembered that she couldn't. Not alone. Desperately she reached up to try, and could reach only the top four buttons. The tightly fitting bodice wouldn't be budged further than that, and after a few minutes of stretching vainly, her arms ached.

She sat down on the bed. What on earth did she do now? There was no question of waking either of the women; it was past one o'clock in the morning. Luke was the obvious choice, and she had just walked out on him, leaving him to drink himself into a stupor. She went and opened her door, biting her lip. Did she go down as if nothing was wrong and ask for help? Something had made him unhappy, and she knew that there had been some sort of quarrel with him and Annabel, and she too was unhappy. Annabel's voice had been too light, her eyes too bright, when she had left.

Then she heard quiet footsteps on the stairs, and her heart leapt. Luke passed the end of the corridor on his way to his own room—if she could ask him now—she saw him, and as she saw him, he looked at her, right from the end of the corridor. Janna half turned, and gestured towards the back of her dress.

He walked silently towards her room, and she whispered: 'My dress—I can't undo the buttons.'

Luke came in and closed the door. 'How clever,' he said. 'How very clever——' The look in his eyes held mockery, and—something else. Something that made her heart beat faster in sudden alarm.

CHAPTER ELEVEN

SHE backed away from him and he said harshly: 'I can't help you if you walk away from me.'

'What do you mean—very clever?' she whispered.

'Why, nothing,' he answered. 'What *could* I mean?'

'I don't know. I don't like you when you're like——'

'There's a shame,' he drawled. 'So why don't you turn round and let's get it over with?' He looked angry. He looked as though he hated her, as though he wanted to hurt her. For an instant she was reminded of the time, high on the mountain road far away, when he had chased after her and struck her in a fury of anger and despair. He looked dangerous enough to do that now.

His mother's room was at the end of the corridor, round the corner. If she screamed she would wake—but there was no way Janna would ever do that. Whatever battle was here concerned no one else, particularly not the kind woman who had opened her home to a perfect stranger.

The awful thing was that she didn't know *why*. Luke's deep dark anger was under control, but only just. It was like a potent force reacting out to stifle her—he stood, hands loosely at sides, in the stance of someone about to fight—ready for defence. Didn't he know she was the one who needed defence? She who had no power to fight him, and was suddenly very afraid. She remained where she was, trembling inwardly. 'It doesn't matter,' she whispered. 'Please go.'

'Not now. Not until I've done what you asked me in for,' he said, equally quietly, and his words were double-edged. Dear God, she thought, he thinks I want him to make love to me.

That was the last thing on her mind. Since meeting Annabel, she had scrupulously avoided any thoughts of that nature, had almost managed to erase them from her memory. Almost. 'I don't want you to touch me,' she said. 'I want you to go.'

'Why did you call me?' He walked slowly towards her, then stopped, only a foot or so away, and looked down at her, big and dark and with such power and anger radiating from him. If he struck her now——She backed away, and she was near the wall. There wasn't much further to go.

'Not for—not for—what you think.' Her eyes were wide with fear. Her heart thudded.

'And what did I think?' he taunted. 'Do tell me, Janna.'

She shook her head. With a movement so swift that she couldn't foresee it, he grabbed hold of her. 'Tell me,' he grated. His fingers dug into her arms, and she winced.

'You're hurting me—let me go, Luke—please——'

'When you've told me.'

'No. I—thought—you thought I'd asked you here to m-make——' She couldn't go on.

'Make love? Was that it? Is that what you were going to say? Is that what you want?' And when she didn't answer, he shook her. 'Is it?' His voice was husky, almost a whisper.

'No——' She shook her head wildly from side to side. 'No!'

'But you did before—you wanted me——'

She whimpered, helpless, sobbing. 'Before—yes, now—no, not any more, not ever again——'

'I want you,' he cut in. 'I want you so much it's driving me insane!'

'No! How can you? There's Annabel—you love her——' The words died in her throat as she saw what was in his eyes. She felt her legs buckle beneath her. This was a nightmare—a waking nightmare. How could he? Was he so beyond all decency that he could desire her, want to possess her when the woman he loved was only minutes away?

'Please, Luke,' she said. 'Please—you don't know what you're saying——'

'I know very well,' he said. 'Oh God, I know only too well. You're sending me insane!'

She went limp, her whole body numbed, her head swirling in a dizzy mist, and Luke took her in his arms, held her to him, and began to undo the buttons at the back of her dress, pulling them, tugging, until they were undone. She struggled free with the last vestiges of her strength, and he said, 'Take it off.'

'No!' She backed away, clutching it.

'Take it off, or by God, I'll tear it off.' He meant it. Trembling, she eased it off, and stood there in the long slim petticoat that Annabel had lent her.

'Satisfied?' she quavered.

'Satisfied? Not yet——' He took her, caught her, and kissed her savagely, all the pent-up anger of him expressed in the violence of the brutal, bruising kiss, and she knew she was going to faint. She could see the light blurring, feel the carpet shifting and swaying beneath her feet, and then merciful oblivion.

When she came round she was lying on the bed, and Luke was sitting by her, leaning over her, rubbing her hands. She opened her eyes and made a little sound of pain, deep in her throat. His face was agonised, and he had gone white. He looked ill. Her fear ebbed away. 'Luke,' she whispered.

He looked at her and his face changed. He looked older, as if the last few minutes had aged him. 'Forgive me,' he said. 'Forgive me——' His voice broke, and he bent forward and rested his head on her breast. He was trembling in the aftermath of his dreadful anger.

'Oh, Luke,' she whispered, and put up her hands to cradle him to her. This tormented man was no danger now. 'It's all right, I'm sorry I made you so angry—but I didn't mean—honestly—I didn't ask you—for that.'

'I know,' his voice was muffled. 'Oh God, I know——'

She lay, feeling the weight of him against her, yet she felt the stronger one. Her hands stroked his hair, his neck, and she had stopped trembling now; she wanted only to reassure him, to comfort him, to let him see that she understood.

He had taken too much drink, and something had upset him, and he had quarrelled with Annabel, and Janna had been there, the scapegoat, to be punished. No more than that. 'It's all right,' she whispered. 'I understand.'

'No, you don't,' he answered.

'But I do.' She laughed softly, reassuringly. 'You

must go now, love. It's late. You'll feel better after a good night's sleep.'

Luke lifted his head. 'Will I?' he said.

His face was only inches away, his breath warm, faintly whisky-scented. 'Yes,' she said. Her eyes were gentle as she looked into his and saw the pain there. 'You'll see.'

Very, very gently he moved, and kissed her mouth, and Janna, knowing that it was just the gesture of apology, seeking forgiveness, kissed him in return. It was a beautiful kiss, full of tenderness and warmth—such a contrast to that savagery of before. Such a contrast.

Luke slid his arms behind her head, and the kiss changed. It was still wonderful, and gentle, but it had changed, become deeper. She couldn't help herself, nor the response he awoke in her. Her soft mouth opened to his, and she heard him groan, then his arms tightened round her, and the warmth was growing, growing, until it filled her. She felt her love welling up inside her, and knew the heady strength of him that had no violence any more, but was transferred to her, along with his caressing hands that had now moved, and were touching her, stroking her, in wonder and delight and pleasure.

'Luke, Luke——' she whispered, in the darkness, as he reached to switch off the light, and he stood up and she heard the soft sounds as he undressed, then lay beside her. 'No, Luke, I——'

His mouth silenced her. His hands delighted her, filled her with sweet treacherous longing and warmth, and his murmured words would have no protest from her. She gave herself up to the wild torment of ecstasy, sobbing at her own betrayal, but lost in the wonder of her senses as he aroused her and himself to fever pitch. All was touch, sweet touch, softness against hardness, gentleness against passion. There was no going back now, there could not be, for all else was forgotten. The only sounds were the sounds of their breathing, quickened, shallow, almost breathless, intense. . . .

Their excitement filled the room, rocked it, until the air vibrated with it, and the darkness was intense, and neither could see, but they didn't need to see, for what was happening needed no light, only the soft warm darkness that sheltered them and gave them the privacy they needed, nearly as much as they needed each other. They were swept along in a pulsing rhythm of mounting excitement and joy and mutual need. For him, for her, there could be no turning back. What had begun in anger and violence and despair was transmuted into an act that was wonderful and wholly beautiful and would only go on, and on, for ever, for ever. . . .

At last they slept, exhausted, fulfilled completely and entirely, and all was quiet and still.

Janna woke while it was still dark, and Luke had gone. Sleepily she turned on her side, and fell into a deep dreamless slumber. The next time she woke up, the sun streamed in through the slightly open curtains, and it was nearly eleven. With her waking came the realisation, and the memories, and she lay there, reliving them at first in wonder and then, gradually, with a growing sense of remorse and shame. She had betrayed the woman Luke loved. How could she ever face her again? Tormented, Janna put her face into the pillow and wept. She wanted to die, for only then would she be free of him. She could not blame him. She blamed only herself. If she hadn't held him when she had seen his despair—if she hadn't responded—if—if—but she had.

Shakily, she got out of bed. Dear Lord, where

would she go? She couldn't stay here, not now. No longer could she tell herself that she was safe, for if she could betray her own promises to herself once, she would do it again. She went over to her chest of drawers to find clean underwear, opened the drawer at the top, and there, folded neatly, were her old trousers, the ones she had worn on the fateful journey, at the beginning. She had opened the wrong drawer. She was about to close it when a fragment of memory returned. Brother Marcos, at the Mission——

She lifted them out and felt in the pocket, pulses hammering, shocked at forgetting something so vital. She drew out a folded piece of paper and smoothed it open. There, written, was the address he had given her and made her promise to contact. She had completely forgotten. She read it carefully, then began her plans.

Janna sat back in the taxi that had taken her away from Courthill. Her mouth was dry, and her head ached.

It was nearly three o'clock on that warm Saturday afternoon, and the only person who knew she had left was Matty. Janna recalled again the scene in the kitchen only an hour previously. Luke was out, and so was his mother. She and Matty were alone in the house, and ever since lunch, which had been eaten by the two of them, Matty had watched her anxiously, and at last asked: 'What is it, child?'

It had all come pouring out. Janna, knowing she could trust the kindly old woman, had told her that she was leaving—because she had fallen in love with Luke, and knew it was wrong, because of Annabel, and must go.

'But where will you go, love?' Matty had asked, her eyes troubled.

'I've got an address given me by someone—a friend. I'll go there. I don't think it's too far away. Have you got a map?'

'There's one in Luke's study. I'll get it for you.' The old lady had hurried out, to return with a map, and Janna, who had memorised the name of the village, looked it up. It was, according to the map, a mere fifteen miles away. She closed it quickly before the old woman could see the page, and looked up.

'How much will a taxi cost me for a journey of about fifteen miles?' she asked.

'Bless you, love, I haven't a clue. A few pounds, I should think.'

She had that. She had changed her precious money at Heathrow, and it came to fifteen pounds. Matty looked at her. 'Don't leave,' she said. 'Talk it over.'

'I can't.' Janna shook her head. 'It's best. I'll leave a note for Luke—and for his mother, of course. When will they be back?'

'Oh, another hour or more—I don't know about Luke. He went out after breakfast, and never said. Oh, Janna, Janna, tell me where you're going.'

Janna shook her head. 'I'll phone, I promise. Luke may find something out next week, but I won't tell him where I am.'

'He'll be worried. He's brought you all this way——'

'I know, and I'll be extremely grateful to him, and I'll pay him back just as soon as I can, but we—we can't—I can't stay—don't you *see*, Matty?'

The old woman nodded. 'Oh aye, I see right enough. He's not—he's been different since you

came, I see that—and you know how fond I am of
Annabel.'

'So am I,' said Janna wretchedly. 'She's been
very kind. That's why I have to go.' She stood up
and hugged the old woman. 'I've packed. Will you
let me have two pieces of paper, please? And will
you phone for a taxi?'

Matty nodded slowly, reluctantly. 'I suppose.'

Janna's mind was clear. The friends lived in a
small village called Frenby and it was outside a
larger town, according to the map. She had asked
the driver to drop her in the town. In the unlikely
event of Luke phoning the taxi firm to check where
she had gone, he wouldn't find out. But it was unlikely, because the greatest feeling on his part would
probably be of relief. . . .

'Nearly there, miss,' the driver turned his head
slightly. 'Where do you want dropping?'

'Is there a bus station?'

'Yes. Next to the market square.'

'Drop me there, will you, please?' She had the
telephone number of Brother Marcos's friends. She
would phone them first. They were unlikely to be
out, because the man was a priest—at least she assumed so; Brother Marcos had written 'The Re-
verend James Miller, The Old Rectory, Frenby.'

She had the paper, with their telephone number
on, in her bag. She had packed her case, taking only
her own possessions in it. All the clothes that Luke
had bought, and the dress that Annabel had given
her, she had left behind all neatly. She had no right
to any of them, particularly not Annabel's dress. All
she had to remind her of Luke was the wedding ring
that hung on the leather thong with the crucifix
round her neck. She felt no bitterness about what
had happened to make her leave, only sadness. She

loved him truly, and wanted him to be happy. He couldn't be while she stayed.

She paid the driver, and twenty minutes later, after a telephone call, was on a bus to Frenby.

The Rectory was just on the outskirts of the village, next to the church, and the driver obligingly dropped her off outside, looking at her curiously as he lifted down her case. 'All right, love?' he asked.

'Yes, thank you very much.' She took the case from him and smiled.

She watched the bus drive away and then turned towards the wooden gate. A woman was walking down the path towards her, a grey-haired, plump, middle-aged woman who was smiling in welcome.

'Janna?' she asked.

'Yes.' Janna put down her case and they shook hands. 'It's very kind of you, Mrs Miller, to have me.'

'My dear, we had a letter from Marcos last week, telling us all about you and insisting we let him know how you were—and we hadn't a clue what he was talking about! Do come in, the kettle's on. My husband won't be back for an hour or so, or he would have come for you in the car, of course——'
She chattered on as they walked up the narrow path of the long garden, filled with flowers. The Rectory was old and of mellowed red brick, a charming house with windows open to the afternoon sun, and an air of peace about it.

Mrs Miller took Janna into a cluttered kitchen and said: 'Tell me why you've come, my dear. You look as though you need our help.' She bustled about, filling the teapot, her actions unhurried. In a way, she reminded Janna of Matty. There was the same air of warmth and kindness about her. Janna knew she had done the right thing.

She began to explain the situation as briefly as possible. It seemed disloyal in a way to Luke, and she didn't want to be that, but otherwise the woman would wonder at her reasons for leaving a place she had spent a week in. She was easy to talk to, her face kindly as she listened, and when Janna had finished she said: 'You're welcome to stay here as long as you wish. Our daughter is married now, and our son is away at university and the house is too big. You've come to the right place, my dear. Marcos is a very old friend of my husband's—even though our religions are different—and he's done us many good turns in the past.'

'You're very kind. Do you know if I'll get a job in the village? I want to work.'

'We'll see. My husband has a solicitor friend whose secretary has left. Can you type?'

'No, but I can learn.'

Mrs Miller laughed. 'I'm sure you can! Drink your tea, then I'll show you your room. I was just going to answer Marcos's letter. He's a good man, a dear soul. I'll be able to tell him you're here.' She looked at the clock on the wall. 'James will be in soon. He was as puzzled as I over Marcos's letter. He'll be delighted to meet you.' She beamed happily at Janna, watched her drink her tea, then stood up. 'Come on, my dear, let's get you settled in.'

The next few days passed quickly. Janna worked hard, helping Mrs Miller in the large house, and pleased to do so. It enabled her not to have to think too much. She wanted to telephone Matty, to see if there was any news, but she was frightened to do so in case Luke answered the phone. On the following Thursday, when Mrs Miller had gone out to visit a sick parishioner Janna stood in the hall of the Rectory, and looked at the telephone. Mrs Miller had assured her she could use it any time she wished, but so far she had resisted the urge. Now, she wanted to. Matty would probably be preparing lunch in the kitchen. Picking it up, she dialled the telephone number she had memorised, and it rang out only once before it was picked up and Matty's voice said: 'Hello.'

'Matty? Matty—it's me, Janna.'

'Janna? Oh, love, where are you? Luke's been——' There was an abrupt silence and then Luke's voice:

'Janna? For God's sake tell me where you are! I——'

Panicking, feeling the blood drain from her head, Janna slammed the receiver down. She stood trembling by the telephone for a few moments, unable to move, her mouth and throat dry with fear. He had sounded terribly angry. She walked from the hall into the kitchen and sat down. She felt faint and sick. She shouldn't have called. She had made a big mistake. Her head pounded, and she put her face in her hands and sat very still for what seemed a long time. She heard a sound, and looked up to see Mrs Miller watching her.

'Oh! I didn't hear you come in,' she said, startled.

'What is it, my dear? You're as white as a sheet.'

'I telephoned, and—he answered. He sounded angry and I panicked and hung up.'

'You should let them know you're safe, you know. Shall I ring for you, Janna?'

She shook her head. 'No. Thank you it's all right.'

'Are you sure?' Mrs Miller sat down and took her hand. 'Oh, you poor thing! Your hand's as cold as ice. Let me get you a nice cup of tea.' It was her solution to any problem—a nice cup of tea. Janna managed a weak smile.

'I'd love one.'

'There now, of course you would.' Mrs Miller patted her hand briskly and stood up. 'Are you sleeping all right, Janna? You're looking a mite peaky. We're feeding you well enough, aren't we? You must say so if not.'

'Oh, yes!' Mrs Miller's cooking was good simple fare, and plenty of it. 'You're a wonderful cook, truly—only I've not felt hungry——'

'Janna.' Mrs Miller sat down again. 'You are—all right, aren't you?'

Janna looked up. Something in the other's voice was odd. 'What—do you mean?' she asked.

'I mean—you couldn't be having—a baby, could you?'

Janna gazed at her in horror. She opened her mouth to answer, then closed it again. Several things, minor things that hadn't seemed of any significance, suddenly assumed a different guise.

'Oh, my dear,' the older woman whispered. 'Could you?'

'Yes,' Janna said very quietly. She bit her lip.

Mrs Miller let out a deep sigh. 'I can always tell—even before a doctor can. It shows in your face, somehow. Oh, my dear child, don't look so worried. I've told you, we'll take care of you.' She shook her head. 'Is he—married?'

'No. Engaged.' Janna twisted her hands nervously. 'He mustn't know.'

'But he must!'

'No, please! That's why I left.'

'He has a responsibility to you, Janna, whether he likes it or not.'

'No, he doesn't,' she shook her head. 'It was my fault as much as his.'

Mrs Miller stood up, agitated. 'Fault? It's not a matter of fault, it's a matter of a life—an unborn baby's life. You need support and help.'

Janna sat there, numb and filled with despair. Mrs Miller didn't even know Luke's name, or where he lived. She hadn't asked. But now she would. 'Let me think about it,' she said, to give her time. 'Please, let me think. I don't want to be a burden to you.'

'You won't be. We'll help you, never fear. But he shouldn't get away scot free. Besides, how do you know he doesn't love you?'

'He doesn't.' Janna looked up. 'I know he doesn't. He—hates me.'

'I don't believe that. Well, we'll talk about it later.' The kettle was beginning to boil. 'There's plenty of time.' Mrs Miller, sensing her despair, changed the subject. 'There's lots of time, and you're here, helping me, and jolly glad I am of it, I can tell you. You're a marvel round the house. I don't know how I managed before!' She put a cup of tea in front of Janna, and smiled warmly. 'Get that down you, love.'

Janna needed it. She was getting to like tea, since coming to England. The initial shock was fading. It had been a shock, to have her own faint suspicions—and that had been all they were—confirmed, but she was rallying fast. It was more essential now than ever before that Luke should not know. Let him go ahead and have the marriage annulled. If he didn't know, he couldn't lie.

After tea, Janna went for a walk round the village, and on her way back walked through the churchyard towards the Rectory. The church doors were closed, but not locked, and on an impulse she went inside and sat down. The rows of empty pews stretched away round her. She and Mrs Miller had been busy cutting fresh flowers from the Rectory garden that afternoon, and they were arranged in vases round the church and near the altar, adding a splash of bright colour to the more sombre tones of greys and browns. It was very quiet and peaceful, and Janna thought about her father, and the mother she had never known, and about her childhood. She wondered if she would ever find anyone—or rather, if Luke would. She would have to phone him eventually, but she wouldn't see him. It would be all done by letter or telephone. Now, more than ever, she mustn't see him. There would be problems with Mrs Miller, who felt it Janna's duty to tell Luke and would probably keep trying to persuade her. . . . She sighed. The kindly woman didn't know all the facts, and never would.

The sooner Janna got a job, the better, even if it would only be for a few months. She didn't want to be a burden to anyone. She felt so tired and dispirited, and leaned back in the pew, aching with a sudden loneliness. However kind Mrs Miller was, it was an imposition, having a stranger. She couldn't stay there for ever. Perhaps, until the baby was born, and then, afterwards, a job, somewhere where she could look after a child, and work, living in, a housekeeper or nanny. She would have Luke's child, and he—or she—would be well loved, and she would always have that memory of Luke. . . .

'Janna.' His voice was no surprise to her, because she thought she was dreaming it, and yet it had seemed almost real.

But his footsteps weren't her imagination. They

were real, and she looked round, and he was walking towards her from the door. She put her hand to her head. Was she dreaming?

He came and sat beside her. His face was very serious, shadowed in the cool evening light. 'Why did you run away?' he asked.

'Did she phone you?' Janna asked.

'Who? Mrs Miller? No. I've been searching for you since Saturday—since you left in that taxi. I called them, and they said they'd dropped you in the market town at the bus station.' He sighed. 'Then I phoned Luis in Rio d'Oro and asked him to get someone to Brother Marcos at the Mission, because I remembered you'd told me that he'd given you the address of some friends. I got Luis's phone call just half an hour ago, and I set off here right away. I've been waiting for you in the Rectory, talking to Mr and Mrs Miller.'

'You shouldn't have come,' she said quietly. 'I explained it all in my letter.'

'No, you didn't. You didn't tell me you loved me. Matty told me that.'

'She shouldn't have done!'

'She did, because I made her tell me.'

'Then you'll know also why I left. I only want you to be happy. You weren't with me, there, I could see that.' She turned her face towards him, eyes bright with tears.

'My dearest girl, don't you know why? Can't you guess?' he said brokenly.

'No, you love Annabel—and I couldn't bear to deceive her any more.'

'I love you, Janna. Only you.'

'How can you say that?'

He cupped her face in his hands. 'Because it's the simple truth, and the only way I know how to say it.

I've loved you desperately almost from the first moment we met—and I fought it, equally desperately, because you were too young. You're not twenty, and I'm so much older——Oh God, don't you know I would give my life for you?' He moved away and put his head in his hands. 'I went to see Annabel on Saturday, to tell her—I could no longer go on living a lie. I knew I had to find you, but first, I had to tell her.'

'Oh, Luke——' She put her arm round him. 'Oh, Luke!'

'She—wait, Janna, you don't know yet. We talked—and then she told me something I was too blind to see. She loves Mark, Janna. I suppose she always has—and he loves her. That was why, when you came——' He stopped.

A beautiful light dawned. 'Annabel and Mark—— Oh!'

'They didn't want to hurt *me*, would you believe. When I told her—when she knew that I loved you, she hugged me. She was laughing and crying, all at the same time——' He paused. 'Only I thought I'd lost you. When you phoned this morning, and then hung up, I was frantic with worry. I'd been waiting for Luis to call. I snatched the phone off Matty— and you put your phone down. Oh God, Janna, I had so much to tell you——'

Janna cradled him to her instinctively, her heart bursting with love. There was something she had to tell him as well, but it could wait. 'It's all right,' she whispered. 'It's all right, love.'

'Your mother had a sister. She lives in Australia. I've got my other brother Bob working on it, from that end. We'll find her, Janna, don't worry, and when we do, we'll go there together. I'm not letting you out of my sight again.'

'Oh, Luke have you? And my father? Any-thing——'

'Only—I know why he went, Janna. I must tell you—he was in an accident, two years before you were born, a car crash, someone was killed and he blamed himself because he was the driver——' He stopped.

She shuddered. 'Oh—no! I knew there was something——'

'But don't you see, my darling, he saved so many lives in the years that followed. He was a good man—you must always remember that. I've got people working on the case now, tracing any re-latives. You'll soon have a family of your own.' He kissed her. 'I must have been a swine to you that past week at my home. And then, on Friday, after the dance—when you'd been dancing with young what's-his-name——'

'Who?' Her mind was a blank.

'The young fellow. Damien something——'

'Oh, *him*!' She dimly remembered a tall young man of about twenty who had taken her off for a few dances. 'I'd forgotten.'

'You'd forgotten! God, I didn't. I saw the two of you together, and it was like—I don't know. I was angry, and jealous—I was like a child. I hated myself, and you.'

'Oh, Luke, I didn't even *see* him. How could I, with you there? Only you were with Annabel—or so it seemed.'

He laughed. 'What a hell of a mix up. Now you know what a jealous, possessive swi——' He looked round. 'Sorry, I forgot where we were. I can't swear in here. Let's go outside.'

'Why? Do you want to swear at me?' she asked mischievously.

'No. I want to tell you certain things I can't in here—about the effect you have on me.' He hugged her. 'I love you so much,' he added softly. 'I always will.'

'And I love you too, with all my heart. Luke—before we go, there is something else——' She paused.

'What is it?' He kissed her, and then looked at her, smiling.

'We—wouldn't be able to get our marriage annulled,' she said softly.

'I have no intention of doing so, you idiot!'

'No, I mean we *couldn't*. I mean——' She began to smile. 'I'm trying to tell you something very simple, and—I can't.'

The smile faded slowly. 'Janna, are you trying to tell me that you're—you're——'

'Yes, Daddy, I am!' She giggled. 'You should see your face!'

'My God, are you all right?' Luke clutched her hand, his face white. 'Do you feel well, my darling? Are you——'

'I'm fine now. Honestly. Say that you don't mind?'

'Mind?' He threw back his head and his laughter echoed round the sombre stone walls. 'Mind? I'm dazed—bewildered—delighted!' He hugged her to him. 'Come on home with me, my darling, now, tonight. Come on home where you belong—with me.' He kissed her. 'For ever and ever.'

Masquerade
Historical Romances

Intrigue excitement romance...

Masquerade is an enthralling series of Historical Romances. As you read you will be transported back to an age of true romance . . . to the courts of eleventh-century Spain . . . to Regency England. From secret assignations in secluded country lanes to high intrigue in glittering chandelier-lit ballrooms.

You will lose yourself in a world where the smile of a beautiful woman could change the course of history.

Every month Masquerade offers you two new romances set against authentic historical backgrounds.

You'll find them where paperbacks are sold.